THE
AMBASSADOR'S
WIFE

THE AMBASSADOR'S WIFE

GLORIA WHELAN

04-178

SERVANT PUBLICATIONS
ANN ARBOR, MICHIGAN

Vine Books is an imprint of Servant Publications.

This is a work of fiction. Apart from obvious references to public figures, places, and historical events, all characters and incidents in this novel are the product of the author's imagination. Any similarities to people living or dead are purely coincidental.

Published by Servant Publications
P.O. Box 8617
Ann Arbor, Michigan 48107

Cover photographs: palm trees by B. Ross/Westlight and flag by R. Watts/Westlight.
Used by permission.
Cover design: Diane Bareis

97 98 99 00   10 9 8 7 6 5 4 3 2 1

Printed in the United States of America
ISBN 1-56955-005-0

LIBRARY OF CONGRESS CATALOGING-IN-PUBLICATION DATA

Whelan, Gloria.
The ambassador's wife / Gloria Whelan.
    p.   cm.
ISBN 1-56955-005-0
I. Title.
PS3573.H442A53   1997
813'.54—dc21   97-12320
                                                      CIP

For Amous

1

As she walked out into the garden of the American ambassador's residency, Jean Pierce could see the gardens of the neighboring homes, gardens that blossomed and leafed with an almost frightening lushness. Although she had lived in tropical countries for years she never quite got used to so much excess. It sometimes seemed that the vines and tendrils of the tropical plants would extinguish the very air she breathed. Adding to the suffocating atmosphere were the high walls dividing the homes, walls festooned with scrolls of razor wire. Their neighbors were government officials too, or businessmen, all targets of assassinations and kidnappings, for Costa Dora was not a peaceful country. In the years since Jean and Dan Pierce had been stationed here, they had witnessed revolutions and military coups. It was only in the last year that there had been some hope of democratic elections. Jean knew how important a part Dan was playing in bringing them about.

Jean held her breath as her husband and son followed her out on the terrace. She had planned to have dinner there instead of in the formal dining room, relying on the informal setting to discourage the usual quarrels between her son and her husband. But the moment Dan and Steve were seated at the table across from one another, any hope for a pleasant meal glimmered and died.

Their loud angry voices seemed out of place as the flowers' fragrance drifted over them in heady waves. The arguments ceased briefly when the servants moved to remove one course and present another. Since these were the two people in her life Jean loved most, it was torture for her to hear their quarrels. But it had been going on for years, going on since Steve was a university student. Now he was a professor, but his adolescent need to challenge his father's position had not changed.

"It's the human condition, Steve," Dan was saying. "In these countries, some years are better than others. That's about the best you can hope for. You think with just a little help from a government—or better still a revolution—you can have a perfect world, heaven on earth. The trouble with you, Steve, is that that university you teach in isn't the real world."

Steve bristled. "I suppose you think ambassadors shuttling between the fortified walls of their residencies and the barricaded walls of their embassies understand the real world. What do you know about the lives of the farm workers who owe most of their harvest to greedy landowners, or the people who are crowded into factories—including children who ought to be in school? You're supporting a corrupt government."

"As American ambassador to Costa Dora, my job is not to reform the country but to represent my own country. What you have to realize, Steve, is that all governments and all leaders, just like all people, have their share of good and evil. Only the proportions differ. Good men can become evil, and evil men good. At the moment a good man is ruling Costa Dora, a man committed to human rights."

"Dad, you know how indecisive he is. The hope that there will be elections is ridiculous. The country is in turmoil. It's only a matter of months before there's a coup. The question is, who will succeed him, the military or the guerrillas? I happen to think the guerrillas would do a better job."

"Thank heaven, those two are not the only options. There's a very good man running in the election. He has a chance of winning."

"I know that man's background. He's a bully."

"He's changed, Steve. People do change."

"Please stop it!" Jean said, a plea that silenced both men. She was close to tears. She had been so pleased to hear that Steve was coming to Costa Dora. He taught Spanish literature at a university in Michigan, a world away from Central America. Jean and Dan seldom saw Steve and his wife, Sarah, and their two children. Hoping to change the subject she said, "You're down here to interview José Iberro?"

"Yes." Steve gave her a penitent look. "To interview him and to lure him up to the university next year to give a reading. Just now he's all the rage. Fashion has as much to do with poetry as it does clothes. Which reminds me, you're looking especially attractive." Steve gave her one of his dazzling smiles, and as they began to talk of Sarah and the children the angry words seemed to be forgotten.

Because they followed the Spanish custom of dining late, it was ten before they left the table. The garden was dark except for the guttering candles in their crystal globes. "I'm going to look up Jorgé," Steve said. "It's been a couple of years since I've seen him. We have some catching up to do."

After Steve left, Dan slumped down in his chair, looking glum. "That's the last person he ought to be seeing."

Jean tried to excuse Steve, as she often did. Perhaps, she told herself, too often. "Jorgé is his oldest friend," she said. It was true.

Jorgé was the son of Manuel Garcia, one of the residence's security guards. Years before, when Jean was looking for someone to help with the gardening, Manuel had suggested his son.

"He's *inteligente*, a smart boy," Manuel had said. "He just finished his first year at the university. It is *infortunado* that he has nothing to do in the summer but get into mischief."

And so Jorgé worked five mornings a week in the summer, helping the other gardeners in caring for the residency's lawn and flowers and its pool and tennis court. Jorgé had a quick smile and inquisitive eyes that missed little. He was a handsome boy, tall but still boyish, like a child who gets his growth too soon. In an effort to appear older he wore the hopeful beginnings of a mustache.

Shortly after Jorgé arrived that first summer, Steve went out to help him move an unwieldy shrub. They were the same age and had become friends, spending their evenings together going to soccer matches or hanging out at the university cafés drinking their Gallo beer.

Because of Jorgé's friendship with Steve, the Pierces had taken Jorgé with them to help with the gardening when they went to the old capital on vacation. There he became a part of the family. Steve, who had always been aloof from the sons and daughters of embassy personnel, seemed at last to have found a friend in Costa Dora.

It was that unique friendship that kept Jean and Dan from remarking on how irked they were that Jorgé regarded them and anything to do with the embassy with a superior and denigrating attitude. They soon found out why he acted the way he did. Manuel had confided to Dan that Jorgé was involved with a Marxist group at the university.

When the Pierces invited Jorgé to a Fourth of July celebration at the residence, Jorgé turned up in jeans and a shirt. Then he made fun of Steve's gray slacks and blazer. Jean and Dan knew Jorgé possessed appropriate clothes, for he dressed suitably on the evenings when they took him with Steve to restaurants.

Steve thought Jorgé's performance amusing, and said he'd change into jeans as well. "You'll do nothing of the kind, Steve," Dan cut in, irritated. "And Jorgé, you put on something appropriate of Steve's, or you can skip the reception."

Jorgé had said, "I will skip the party. Why should I dress up for a celebration of a country that fights for liberty for itself, yet turns its back on the people in my country who fight for liberty?" Steve agreed and refused to go as well. After that night Jean and Dan had seen less and less of Jorgé, but they knew that over the years Steve wrote to Jorgé and kept up his friendship.

* * *

Later that evening when Steve returned home, Jean and Dan were already asleep. In the morning over their coffee, Jean asked, "How was Jorgé?"

"He hasn't changed," Steve said. "He's ready to join any revolution that comes along."

Dan gave Steve a long look. "That wouldn't be a smart thing to say outside of the confines of this room, Steve."

"That I can't say something like that in public proves there isn't freedom in this country."

"I'm not talking about censorship, Steve. I'm talking about diplomacy. An ambassador's son can't be seen running around supporting anti-government forces."

"But I'm not just 'the ambassador's son.' I have a right to express my own opinion."

Jean was trying to think how to avert another argument when Rosa, the residency housekeeper, appeared. Rosa had been with them as long as they had been in Costa Dora. She was a small, round woman with a perpetual smile and a thick braid that reached her waist. She was proud of her small feet, and wore high heeled shoes in bright colors to do even the most rigorous household work. On this morning her smile was strangely absent as she excused herself.

"Señor Pierce," she said. "I'm sorry to bother your breakfast, but Manuel must see you at once."

Dan looked up, surprised. Throwing down his napkin he followed Rosa from the room. Watching Dan, Jean thought how strange it was that this authoritative ambassador was also her husband, a man she knew to be as human and frail as any person. She saw the toll these arguments with Steve took on him. But she knew he was careful not to let Steve see. Turning to Steve now, Jean said lightly, "How about letting up on your father? He's as concerned with the government's injustices as you are. As ambassador, he has to take an official position. But behind the scenes, Steve, he does everything he can to encourage democracy. You're only down here for a week. Why can't we just enjoy being together instead of being at each other's throats?"

Steve grinned at her. "You're right. I'll call a truce. I don't know why I make such a thing of it. This country is no worse than a lot of other Central American countries. I suppose it's just because I've spent so many years here. I guess I have more loyalty to Costa Dora than I do to America. I always felt like an alien in America. I suppose I should start paying attention to American politics. Maybe I can do something there."

"How is Sarah?" Jean was relieved to turn to a neutral subject.

"Wonderful. She loves her job with the archaeology department and she's a natural born teacher. She'd like to work full time, but until Mia and Tim are a little older she's doing a lot of her research at home."

With the conversation in safe territory Jean began to relax, sure that for the rest of the meal arguments would be put aside. She was unprepared for the harried look on Dan's face when he returned.

"What is it?" she asked. "What's happened?"

Dan looked from Jean to Steve. His face was pale. His lips were tightly compressed, as though he were struggling to keep from speaking. He shook his head, signaling some interior decision. "You both might as well know the truth, but it's not to leave this room. Manuel tells me that Jorgé was arrested this morning for something called 'revolutionary activity against the state.' I don't understand it. Jorgé has been on the fringe of activist groups known to oppose the government for years. Why did they pick him up today?"

Jean felt her heart pounding. She looked at Steve. "You were with Jorgé last night. They might have arrested you as well."

Steve's face was flushed, the knuckles on his clenched fists white. He turned a furious face to Dan. "No. I was in no danger. *My* father is the ambassador. Jorgé's father is merely a guard." He gave Dan a withering look. "*This* is the government you're supporting. If anything happens to Jorgé, I hold you responsible." Steve sprang from his chair and strode toward the door.

"Steve," his father called to him. "Leave this to me. You're not to get involved."

Steve looked around. "You can give orders at the embassy, but the days are over when you can order me around."

2

Steve brushed by Rosa and hurried to the car he had rented for his stay. He had not wanted to be dependent on the embassy to get around. As he backed the car out of the guarded gates, he thought about his first meeting with Jorgé when they had worked in the residency garden together. Jorgé had been at the *Universidad de Costa Dora* then. "I never bother with classes," Jorgé had boasted. "I have more important things to do." He was alert, excited, and full of tales of his new comrades who intended to wrest the government away from the "army fascists."

Jorgé's enthusiasm had made Steve envious. He told himself that while he was slogging away in North America over an abstract thesis about obscure authors that no one would ever bother to read, Jorgé would be involved in the real world, in things that might change lives.

Proudly Jorgé had introduced Steve to his friends from the university. At first the students were hostile. They resented the fact that Steve was American. And though he never mentioned his last name and tried to hide the fact that his father was the ambassador, still he was an American. At that time the country was going through a chaotic period. The currency had lost half its value. Export prices for sugar and coffee had dropped. Unemployment was endemic. And though the army, which had been responsible for years of kidnappings and massacres, had allowed an election, it was far from democratic. The army was insisting that the new president agree to give the government soldiers amnesty, a plan the guerrillas violently opposed. The United States had sided against the guerrillas. So to the guerrillas Steve was one of the despised *nortéamericanos.*

Steve had been quick to let the students know that he didn't approve of American policy. Then Carlos, one of the leaders of the group, took an interest in Steve. Jorgé was impressed. "He's been up north," Jorgé had said. "Up north" was the euphemism used in the group for those who had spent time in the guerrilla camps on Costa Dora's northern border. When the army went after the members of the guerrilla forces, the guerrillas fled over the border, then waited until it was safe to return again.

Carlos singled Steve out and took Jorgé and Steve to late night student hangouts on the small *avenidas* where *mariachi* bands down from Mexico played their frenetic music. It turned out Carlos had known all along what Steve's father did.

"What goes on behind those embassy doors?" Carlos asked casually one night.

Steve had spent too many years living among his father's secrets to give away confidential information. Instead he described the dull routine interrupted by even duller parties. But it seemed no detail was too small for Carlos's attention. "Who comes to the parties?" Carlos wanted to know. What local businessmen? What generals? What officials? To whom did they talk? Who was friendly with whom? What had seemed unimportant chitchat to Steve appeared of great interest to Carlos. Steve had been impressionable, flattered that Carlos, who seemed to be a leader of the activists among the students, trusted him. He knew Carlos was pumping him for information, but that was Carlos' duty. Steve believed he was not divulging secrets but simply describing parties. Besides, whatever information he gave about the embassy would be used for a good cause, a cause in which Steve had grown to believe.

It was nearly the end of that summer when Carlos allowed Jorgé to take Steve to a secret meeting. A well-known Marxist spoke about the need to take over the country and give the land to the peasants. Then someone accused the military of atrocities. Songs were sung, pledges made. Steve was exhilarated. He had always regretted missing the sixties, the years of protest and rebellion. At the activists' meeting he felt at last he was in touch with the real world.

That night Steve had returned to the residency after midnight. Intoxicated with revolutionary zeal, Steve had given the clenched fist salute to Manuel, sure that Manuel and all the workers in Costa Dora were eager to take to the streets and follow Carlos and his comrades.

Instead Manuel had turned on Steve. "You and Jorgé are fools, no better than children. You are safe because of your father, but my son could end up in jail or worse. Better you stay away from those *perros.*" Steve remembered being taken aback by Manuel's reaction.

The next morning Steve's father had stuck his head into Steve's room, where Steve was still in bed. "Meet me for lunch at the Café Hapsburg, one o'clock," he ordered.

Instantly Steve bristled. He felt at a disadvantage lying there in bed while his father stood at the door in a business suit. And he didn't like being ordered about. "I'm not sure I can make it," he said.

"Be there," Dan replied. The door slammed.

Shaken, Steve had complied.

The restaurant was located in the city's largest hotel. Steve always marveled at the restaurant's anachronistic attempt in this Central American country, with its Indian and Spanish heritage, to replicate Vienna at the turn of the century. Steve had been ushered to a secluded table where his father was waiting for him.

Dan looked up as Steve pulled out a chair. "I didn't mean to order you around this morning. I was upset."

Immediately Steve was on the defensive. "Are you going to tell me why?"

"I heard about the meeting you attended last night."

"I should have known you'd have your spies there."

Dan bristled. "What do you mean by that remark?"

"I shouldn't have to explain. I'm not a fool. I know the embassy isn't just for teas and dinner parties. I can guess the kind of business you conduct when you're in your office behind closed doors. I can guess what kind of mail goes back and forth to Washington in the diplomatic pouches."

"I'm not ashamed of what I do and neither should you be ashamed of it."

"I think you'll have to leave that up to me."

There was an awkward pause as the waiter came to take their orders. In a small show of agreement they both ordered smoked salmon appetizers.

When the waiter left Dan said, "That meeting was dangerous. The meeting could have been raided, and you and Jorgé might have ended up in jail."

"If we had it would have been for a good cause."

"Those people mean to take over the country using whatever violence it takes."

"I don't suppose your side uses violence?" Steve said with heavy sarcasm.

"What do you mean by 'my side'?"

"I mean the rich landlords who grab even the pocket-sized pieces of land the Maya own. I mean Costa Dora's army that's out there killing people in the villages. The army of a government supported by the United States."

"Don't be naive, Steve. What happens is that the guerrillas start an armed action near an Indian village and then turn tail and run, leaving the Indians to face an angry army. Your men are cowards who want to fight to the last Indian. I don't want you mixed up with the guerrillas."

"What you're worried about is that I could do something to embarrass you."

"I'm thinking about you, Steve, and not myself. The trouble with you is that you're young and impressionable. You think there are easy answers. Just start a revolution and stand back. Meantime thousands are killed and you have a country in chaos."

All Steve heard was his father calling him "young and impressionable." He considered storming out of the restaurant, but at just that moment the waiter arrived to place plates of smoked salmon before them. His father was a regular at the restaurant and the generous portions of salmon were garnished with lemon slices and capers, just as his father liked them. Though he was angry, Steve was also hungry.

In a more conciliatory voice Dan said, "Don't misunderstand me, Steve. I'm not trying to tell you what to think. There's right as well as wrong on both sides. I only want you to be clear about what you're doing and, more important, with whom you're doing it. Achieving democracy is an end with you; for them it's a means to something else."

"Why should I listen to you? We're on different sides."

Dan said sadly, "You make us sound like enemies. Haven't you an overly dramatic view of my work?"

"How could I have? You've never told me exactly what it is you do."

"Let me tell you now. The work is really quite dull, nothing you couldn't do yourself. Ninety percent of it is pushing papers and shaking hands."

"I'd rather not hear about it. I'd just as soon not be associated with what you do."

His father had flushed in anger. "How can you not be? It's put the bread—and the smoked salmon—in your mouth."

Steve dropped his fork and stared at his father, furious.

"I'll admit that was a cheap shot, Steve, but what you've been implying is that I'm some sort of moral leper or a two-bit hoodlum. That's not easy to take from a son. I've done hard things, things I would rather not have had to do, but nothing I'm ashamed of. And a few things I'm rather proud of."

"You're asking me to take what you do on faith, to trust you, yet you won't do the same for me."

"There's a difference. Whatever I've done, I've done with my eyes open. I've known exactly with whom I'm dealing. I'm asking you to do the same. I want you to know if you are being used."

"What does it matter if I'm being used if I help to make a point?"

"After you make your point, they'll make theirs."

"You've been dealing with diplomatic dishonesty so many years, you don't know idealism when you see it."

The rest of their lunch had been consumed in a rush, the salmon forked viciously, the rolls twisted apart in anger, tender slices of veal swallowed in a kind of rage. With no food left to punish, they had stared at each other over their ravaged plates.

"Let's get out of here," his father said.

They walked along the dusty streets, the afternoon sun casting the moving silhouettes of their figures against the walls of the buildings that sheltered large homes. On one corner a man had set up a table of cheap machine-made weavings hoping to attract a tourist or two, though tourists disappeared from Costa Dora in the summer as though climate was the only thing about the country that interested them. The man's family, a wife and four children, sat licking flavored ice cones in the shade of a nearby tree, staring openly at Steve and his father.

"I don't suppose it was all that easy for you, Steve, moving from country to country, not belonging anywhere. I know your mother feels it. If something happened to me, I don't know where she would go."

It had not occurred to Steve that his father thought about "something happening" to him.

"Is there trouble brewing?" he asked, though he was irritated to find himself worrying about his father.

"Not for the moment," Dan said. He gave Steve an ironic smile. "But I don't have to tell you that trouble here is always just around the corner. How about you? You'll be going to graduate school in a month."

"I don't know if I'm going back." Steve hadn't been entirely ready to be conciliatory. "There are some interesting things happening in Costa Dora. I might try an article or two about Costa Dora for one of the papers in the States. My Spanish would help me get information." He returned his father's smile. "We may end up in the same place—on different sides." Steve asked himself who was taking cheap shots now. He waited for his father's anger, but Dan evidently had his own agenda.

"Look, Steve, go back and finish your graduate degree.

Professor Abrabanel told us he thinks the world of you. If you'll do that much we're quits. After that you can do whatever you please. I won't say a word, but I don't want to hear about it from the police, either." He put his arm around Steve's shoulder. "Then if you want to lead a revolution, I'll teach you how."

Steve had agreed. It was nothing his father had said. It was the man's charm. He had no defense against it. So in the fall he went back to the university and met Sarah. When he finished his graduate degree, he and Sarah had been married. Abrabanel offered him an instructorship and he accepted. After that he had lost touch with Jorgé, seeing him only on rare visits to Costa Dora, as he had seen him the night before.

*   *   *

Steve refused to think about his father's admonishing him to do nothing about Jorgé's arrest, to leave it to him. Steve told himself Jorgé was his friend and there was little he wouldn't do to get Jorgé out of the government's clutches. So he headed for the small café Jorgé had taken him to the night before, anxious for any information about the arrest. Carlos had been there that night and had joined them for a drink, saying little and then leaving abruptly.

The café was a shabby building in a crowded working class section of the city. It had once been a beauty parlor. Pink plastic draperies, faded and rotting with age, were strung across the window. The linoleum was pink with flecks of gold and you could see holes in the wall where the sinks had been. Steve walked in, uncomfortably aware that even in jeans he looked out of place. A few people glanced at him and then immediately looked away. It was a place where inquiring glances were not welcome.

Across the room Steve saw Carlos sitting alone. He walked over to the table, and without asking permission, sat down across from Carlos. He leaned over the table and said, "Jorgé …"

Before he could finish the sentence Carlos said, *"Silencio!"* He switched to English. "I know what you are going to say. I have heard." Carlos motioned to the bartender who sent over a waitress with a bottle of the local vodka. Carlos began to talk with him about Jorgé and what might happen to him. "The government people are animals. Right now Jorgé is in some cell. Perhaps there is torture. Who can tell? It would be like them."

Between the two of them they finished a *botella* of the vodka. The drinking was some sort of *machismo* thing. Steve felt he had to keep up, although on some less-conscious level he knew Carlos was letting him do most of the drinking. "What can we do?" Steve asked. "There must be some way of helping him."

Carlos gave Steve a deprecatory look. "It may be possible to do something, but you would not be the one to do it with your sheltered embassy life. What do you know of what we must suffer? You have always gone to expensive schools for American children. Now you live a thousand miles away in an academic world. You come here to dabble in our poetry while your best friend is in a jail cell. You pretend an interest in our struggle but for you it is only a kind of slumming, a sop to your conscience. You have never cared about the revolution."

There was enough truth to what Carlos was saying so that Steve was defensive. "That isn't true. I'd do anything to help Jorgé."

Carlos leaned across the table, his eyes narrowed, his voice became a whisper. "Do you trust me?"

Steve's head ached from the home-distilled vodka. He was

having trouble hearing Carlos. He leaned closer to him. He could smell the man's sweat and the rank odor of garlic on his breath.

"Yes, of course I trust you." All Steve could think of was Jorgé in some jail cell. He was desperate to separate himself from the embassy and its connections with the government that had arrested Jorgé, desperate to show Carlos and the guerrillas that he was on their side. He didn't want Jorgé's blood on his hands. "What can I do?" he asked Carlos. "Just tell me what I can do."

Carlos leaned across the table and began to speak in a soft, insistent voice.

* * *

It was after midnight when Steve returned to the residency. Manuel was on night duty guarding the gate. Steve caught Manuel's tortured face in his headlights. At the gate Manuel turned on him. "I told you and Jorgé to stay away from trouble. Now you see what has come of two children playing at revolution."

Steve was stung at being called a child. "Don't worry," he said. "I promise I'll find a way to free him."

"I don't want any help from you. Stay out of it. I have asked your father's help."

Steve winced, sobered by the contempt in Manuel's voice. He needed to get to his room, to be alone so he could plan his next move, but his mother was waiting for him.

"Your father has gone out. I hope you haven't done anything foolish?"

"I don't know that you and I would have the same definition of foolish," he said bitterly. Steve saw the wounded look on his mother's face. "I'm sorry. I didn't mean to hurt you, but Jorgé's arrest changes everything. I'm going up to my room. Tomorrow I'll drive to the old capital to interview José Iberro. From there I'll go directly to the airport. There's no point in seeing Dad again. We'd only be at one another's throats and I know you hate that."

"But what about Jorgé? Your father was going to see what he could do."

"What can *he* do? Anyhow, there's no need to worry anymore about Jorgé. I've taken care of that."

In two days Steve was flying over Costa Dora on his way home to the States. As he looked down at the miles of green he felt for the first time that he never wanted to see the country again.

3

Dan's driver gave the signal to open the steel gates of the residency. Since the ambassador was not on official business there was nothing to identify his car, a routine security measure in a country where murder and kidnappings were commonplace. Instead, Dan was riding in one of the small Japanese cars so popular in Costa Dora. He was taking a half hour from his busy schedule to visit the embassy's economic officer who was in the hospital recovering from an emergency appendectomy. In spite of the chaotic conditions in Costa Dora the man had been successful in bringing in new American investments to bolster the Costa Doran economy. Dan wanted to show his gratitude.

As the car pulled out of the residency drive Manuel gave Dan a brisk salute. The greeting they exchanged was not that between master and servant but between co-conspirators whose collaboration remained a secret between them—and a bond. Two weeks had passed since Jorgé was imprisoned and two more weeks since he was freed.

Manuel shifted his automatic weapon and closed the gate as the car pulled away. It was not only the Ambassador's residency that was secured. On both sides of the street the entrances of the large homes were patrolled by guards wielding shotguns and even machine guns. The guards were so familiar that residents were not only accustomed to them, but puzzled to see a home without an armed protector. The whole city was a garrison, with a frightened population hunkered down behind steel bars hoping for the election of a new president who would liberate them from roving gangs of thieves, a corrupt government, and the threat of revolution. Until that happened they lived with what people had come to call simply *la violencia*, the violence.

Dan chafed under the extravagant security measures, but not too many years ago one of his predecessors had been gunned down. Lately Dan's worry was not his own safety but his wife's uneasiness. As the tension in the country mounted, Jean was finding small ways to delay his departures. This morning she insisted he talk with someone about one of the chimneys, complaining it was smoking. Too impatiently he had said, "Surely there must be someone on the staff who can see to that. I haven't been sent down here by Washington to clean chimneys." Immediately he had regretted his cross response and apologized. He supposed her worry was a reaction to the increasing publicity about the government's military school. In the last week, newspapers supporting the guerrillas had broken the story that Costa Dora's feared security forces were being trained by American officers. The story had sparked a renewal of violence on the part of the guerrillas and an equally violent retaliation on the part of the government. Jean had said, "You'll be the one to be blamed for any part the Americans have in it. That school has always been a target of the guerrillas. Why must we get involved in the corrupt politics of this country?"

With an effort Dan had made his voice light. "Jean, you're beginning to sound like Steve." Since Steve's abrupt departure two weeks before, Jean's uneasiness had increased. Dan tried to explain. "You know if the government doesn't have a strong security force there will be chaos in this country. The guerrillas would take over and impose a Marxist government. It would be Cuba all over again. What the newspaper didn't bother to say is that by being involved, the United States government has a chance to oversee the local security forces and, believe me, they need watching."

* * *

Secretly, he was alarmed. America's involvement with the training camp had been top secret. Someone high up in the Costa Doran government—or unthinkable, someone in the embassy—had given the secret away in an effort to discredit the United States. As the American ambassador, Dan was the one who was taking the heat. Ironically, he had not approved of the involvement and had fought against it, but in the end he had lost and now it was his job to uphold his country's position. For the thousandth time he was having to deal with the struggle between his own beliefs and those of his government. He wondered what Steve would say if he knew about these struggles; even more he wondered why he had never confessed them to Steve. He had always tried to appear the strong father, a man without doubts or conflicts. Now he was having second thoughts. Why shouldn't he let Steve know that he too had unanswered questions and conflicts? He resolved to write Steve when he got back to the embassy. Just now he was more concerned with Jean's worries.

He had tried to reassure her, "Anyhow, I don't go anywhere without my nanny." His "nanny" was Bruce Miles, who doubled as driver and guard. Bruce had worked for the Secret Service for ten years before being assigned a year ago to the embassy at Costa Dora. The employees at the embassy had taken to calling him "the nanny" because he was a strict disciplinarian, checking out routes, vetting workers hired by the embassy, even high-handedly insisting on the cancellation of Dan's appointments when he believed there was some danger.

Dan and Jean had lived with danger from the start of their marriage. Dan's first post for the State Department had been in Spain at the height of the Basque and Catalan terrorism. Before their present posting they had had a tour of duty in Argentina, enduring Perón's return and the ensuing military coups, kidnappings, and killings. Seventeen years ago he had come to Costa Dora as first secretary and had worked his way up to ambassador, one of the few ambassadors who were not political appointments. Now he looked forward to next year when he would retire. For all the thirty-five years of their marriage, Jean and Dan had lived in the midst of upheaval. In America people turned on their TV and watched pictures of revolution, war, and slaughter—and calmly ate their dinner. After they turned off their TV and went on with their lives, he and Jean were still there in the thick of the chaos.

Long ago he decided that this was the human condition. Some years are better than others, but never for long. He would do all he could to bring about democracy in this volatile country, but nothing in his background made him an optimist. He knew that if there was a perfect world it was not on this earth.

* * *

The city's main boulevard was lined with dusty-leaved trees and decorated with shriveled flower beds less colorful than the accumulating crop of discarded tins and bright paper wrappers. Every corner had its lottery vendor and its beggar. Nearby were upscale hotels, fashionable shops, and the ubiquitous American fast-food restaurants. A small group of protesters carrying banners were gathered in front of a building. *At least people can protest now,* Dan thought. There was a time when a demonstration like that would have meant instant imprisonment and even death.

Bruce turned down a narrow *calle* lined with blossoming jacaranda in sherbet colors of raspberry, grape, and orange. Out of habit Bruce was keeping an eye on the rearview mirror. Now he turned to Dan, his voice tight and low. "Probably nothing to worry about, but there's a car making the same turns we are. I think I'll give the police a buzz."

Dan knew what that meant. The local police loved nothing so much as turning on their sirens. A crowd would gather. One of the police would leak the incident to reporters. For one political reason or another it would be blown up in the newspapers. The government paper would accuse the guerrillas of plotting an assassination while the paper sympathetic to the guerrillas would accuse Dan of manufacturing an incident to discredit them. "It's probably a coincidence," he said. "Let's hold off."

As they approached the cross street, an ancient Crown Victoria, a ghost of the grandiose cars that used to be, pulled in front of them, blocking their way. Lurching over the curb, Bruce tried to swing past the blockade. A wall lined the sidewalk. There was no room. He began backing up but another car was behind him. Bruce's gun was in his hand but they were shut into the car as into a casket. Dan had only time to think fleetingly of Jean.

4

When the phone rang at the residency it was Dan's secretary, Evelyn Seburn, at the embassy, calling to talk with Jean about a dinner the embassy was giving the next night to welcome a congressman from the States. He was coming to Costa Dora on some hush-hush investigation. Jean remembered Dan's worrying about the visit. Without telling her the purpose of the investigation he had shaken his head and complained, "Someone's stirring up trouble in Washington." The official explanation of the visit was an effort by the congressman to increase trade between the two countries.

Evelyn went on about details of the seating for the party and the hiring of a marimba player, details that had already been decided. Puzzled, Jean assured her, "That's all been taken care of, Evelyn, but I appreciate your checking." She was about to hang up but the secretary kept up a nervous stream of talk, odd in someone usually organized and businesslike. There was a slightly hysterical edge to her voice and an insistence on continuing the conversation that alerted Jean. "Evelyn, this has nothing to do with the congressman's visit. What is it?"

There was a long pause. Finally Evelyn answered in a strained voice, "Jim Benkin is on his way over to see you," she said. "Jim and a couple of others. They'll be right there. He has something he wants to talk to you about. He just asked me to tell you so you'd expect him, so you'd be there."

"Of course, I'll be here." Jim Benkin was the first secretary at the embassy. "Evelyn, what is it? Has anything happened in the city?" Recently the guerrillas had been stepping up acts of terrorism, actually creating incidents right in the capital.

Evelyn said, "No, it's not that. It's …," but she had not been able to finish the sentence. Bursting into tears, she apologized, then hung up leaving Jean with a feeling of dread. Jean knew Evelyn was keeping her on the phone for a reason. But why? To keep someone else from getting to her? But who? At the edge of Jean's consciousness the answer was already there. Someone with bad news, with questions. Reporters.

At the sound of cars an alarmed Jean rushed to the window to see the residency gates open to admit two official vehicles. From the first she saw four security officers hastily emerge and take positions outside the house, two supplanting Manuel standing guard at the entrance, guns slung over their shoulders, and two slipping unobtrusively into the shadows.

Frightened, Jean watched as Jim Benkin climbed out of the second car. With him was Elwood Randall, the embassy press officer, and an American physician, Dr. Iverson, who often cared for embassy personnel. Benkin's face was grim and strained, as though his expression had been donned some time before and was already becoming a burden. The doctor appeared businesslike. The press officer wore a trench coat with the belt tied instead of buckled—an affectation Jean remembered Dan ridiculing.

Benkin did not wait for Rosa to usher him into the sitting room but, with the other two men, moved at once through the doorway. For a moment Jean felt they were being rude, which was odd, because Benkin was the most courteous of men. It seemed important that she regain control before whatever was going to happen to her happened. "Please come in, won't you, and sit down?" It was a large room with white walls and crowded bookshelves. There were coarsely woven rugs in bright colors on the dark wood floors. On the shelves and walls was a modest collection of art garnered from the various countries in which Dan and Jean had lived. Bowls of fresh flowers stood on the tables. She wanted to postpone whatever it was they were going to say to her. She tried to think of something to make them comfortable. The morning had been chilly and she now offered, "I could have the fire lighted. It's been set."

Benkin put his arm around her and led her to a small couch. He was a slim, weedy man who was always impeccably dressed. Jean could never recall seeing him without a tie and jacket—even at informal embassy picnics—until this moment. He wore no tie now, and she was startled to see that his socks were mismatched. Then she recalled Dan's having mentioned giving Benkin the day off to move to a new home. More than anything else it was the fastidious Benkin's dishevelment that frightened her.

Benkin sat down beside her and took her hand—another uncharacteristic thing, for Benkin was always a little aloof. His hand was cold. The doctor and the press secretary stood apart, appearing embarrassed at being witnesses to whatever Benkin was going to tell Jean.

"There has been an accident," Benkin said.

Jean looked at the doctor, who stood stiffly at attention as though waiting for an order. Why wasn't the doctor with Dan? Why was he in attendance on her? There must be something more. Like an obedient child she allowed her hand to rest in

Benkin's, but its coldness chilled her. In her distracted state the thought entered her head that for so reticent a man, this personal contact must have cost him a great deal.

"Jean, I'm afraid I must tell you. We don't have much time before the newspapers start calling." He took a long breath. "Dan has been killed."

Jean felt the room tremble under her. For a moment she thought it was an earthquake and then she realized it was her body shaking. She stared angrily at Jim Benkin. What did he mean they "didn't have much time?" If Dan was dead, there was all the time in the world. There was nothing but time. She could not see to the end of it. But they were looking at her. Waiting for her to say something. The odd thought passed through her head that it was impolite of her to remain silent. In a strangled voice she managed to ask, "What happened?"

"Are you all right, Mrs. Pierce?" Dr. Iverson asked, moving closer.

She ignored the fatuous question. Of course she was not all right. "What happened?" she asked again.

Benkin said, "Daniel never reached the hospital. We think Bruce must have had some trouble with the engine. The hood was propped open. Evidently some thugs, seeing that Dan had a driver and guessing he would have money, attacked him."

Randall interposed too quickly: "We think it was a simple robbery. They would have had no idea he was from the embassy. The car didn't have embassy plates. They would have thought with a driver he was a wealthy businessman, someone to rob."

"But why would thieves ... " She could not get the words out.

"Why would they kill him?" Benkin finished for her. "We believe Bruce and Dan struggled with them."

"Are you sure it was Dan?" She could not resist grasping at a last shred of hope.

"I identified him myself," Benkin said. "We thought it would be easier for you. There are always reporters hanging around the ... " This time it was Benkin who could not finish. Jean understood he was about to say "morgue," but he changed it to "police station." "Bruce was killed as well so we will never know exactly what happened."

"But we're convinced it was robbery," Randall insisted. His insistence made Jean suspicious, but she was too dazed to formulate a question.

Benkin went on, his voice slow and insistent as if he were instructing a child. "The reports of the robbery will be bad enough but it would be difficult if just before the election there were the wrong kind of rumors. Some, of course, are inevitable. With your permission, Randall will stay here to handle the phone and the press calls. I'll be at the embassy and you have only to call me for anything you might need. I don't have to tell you how crushed we are. Dan was a good man." When Jean saw tears in Benkin's eyes the coldness of his hand no longer bothered her. She grasped it tightly.

Randall said, "The embassy can arrange to have the body flown to the States. Actually a plane has already been chartered."

Jean shook her head. "We have no home in the States. Dan will be buried here." There was an ancient cemetery in the old capital where they had a small home, a retreat from the formal life of the embassy. The cemetery was a pleasant place with tall trees and a feeling of peace, something Dan had seldom had in his lifetime.

Benkin and the press officer exchanged unhappy glances. Jean realized they had hoped the body, with Jean accompanying it, would leave the country within hours. After that the problem would be out of their hands. With the election coming in Costa Dora, its president would want the whole thing hushed up. He would not want an investigation that might reflect on the state of order in the city. Obviously there would be publicity in the States, but a mugging and killing would hardly be scandalous news there.

"Wouldn't you feel better with your family?" Randall coaxed.

Jean paid no attention to the question. She was thinking that Steve must be told. "I'll have to call my son. Will the embassy help with arrangements for his trip down for the funeral?"

Benkin's resigned sigh suggested he had not expected that things would go according to plan. Still he continued to try. "I suppose you'll be leaving with your son after the funeral? We can take care of that for you. We can close your house here and in the old capital and so forth."

He appeared embarrassed to be rushing her. She only shook her head. She had no intention of being rushed.

Dr. Iverson said, "I could leave a prescription for you, Mrs. Pierce—just to get you through the next days."

Again she shook her head. How could they think a pill of some sort would dull the pain she felt? That kind of pill had not been invented.

Randall said, "I'll just handle the phone and field any calls, Mrs. Pierce. I'll try not to get in your way. I hope I'll be of some help."

Benkin began to follow the doctor and Randall out of the room. Suddenly, when the doctor and Randall were out of sight Benkin turned to Jean. The look of haggard sympathy on his face said he could not keep the truth from her. Impulsively he reached into his coat pocket, handed her Dan's wallet and watch and a cigarette lighter. "I know I can trust you not to say anything." Benkin turned and quickly walked out of the room.

Jean sank into a chair. So it had not been a robbery but an assassination. She found she was not surprised. All these years she had seen violence stalking them like some small, maligned animal waiting to attack. If you were with the State Department you took sides. If you took sides, you made enemies.

The stakes were always high—governments rose or fell on what Dan did. She had always believed he had been on the side of good. Steve had said Dan had no business interfering in the governments of other countries, but Dan always hoped that he could make some small difference.

Her first impulse was to shout out that someone had killed Dan. She wanted to demand justice, punishment, retribution for taking Dan's life. A moment later she could hear Dan's voice telling her she must keep silent about the assassination. She must do what would be best for Costa Dora. With the election coming up she had no right to undo everything Dan had worked for all these years. There was only one person in whom she could confide. When Steve came down she would tell him. Thinking of Steve she willed her body to get up and walk across the room to the telephone. She stood there looking at it, trying to find enough strength to dial Steve's number but it seemed an impossible task.

Rosa was at the doorway, her face streaked with tears. "Oh, Señora," she said. As if the sight of Rosa's tears were a reminder of what she must do, Jean began to cry. She did not think she would ever stop. Rosa took her in her arms and held her and there was no telling whose tears were on whose faces.

5

Steve took the call at the university. A student was with him, discussing a paper she wanted to do on José Iberro's poetry. Steve thought she saw only the beauty of the lyric poems. He had been trying to get her to look more deeply, to see the message of suffering behind Iberro's lovely lines, but he decided she was too young to dwell on sorrow and disappointment. With a sigh he thought, *Let it go. She will have plenty of time for that. Why destroy her lighthearted optimism?*

He excused himself and reached for the phone.

"When?" he asked weakly. "I can't believe it. What happened? Are you all right? Mother, I'm so sorry. I wish I were there with you. I'll get the first plane out. Leave everything to me." He hung up and turned to the student. In his own sorrow, Steve did not spare her. "That was my mother," he said. "My father has been killed in a brutal robbery."

The young girl looked up at his devastated face, at the tears that he was unsuccessfully trying to blink back. Helplessly she said, "It's like that line of Iberro's: 'We are all hung on the cross and our hands joined.'"

Steve looked at her, startled. So she had known about suffering all along.

By the time Steve reached his home he was shaken but very

much in control of himself. He refused Sarah's offer to accompany him. "No point to it, Sarah. There's the expense, and you'd have to find a substitute to teach your classes at the university. And we'd have to get someone to care for the children. I'll be back right after the funeral, and I'm sure Mother will want to return as soon as things get straightened out there. I can't think why anyone would live down there if they didn't have to. If you have a corrupt government you will have *la violencia.*"

At the word "violence" Sarah asked, "You won't be seeing your friends while you're down there?" It was more of a request than a question.

Steve gave her a quick look. He knew whom she meant. "No. There won't be time for that, but there's no reason I *shouldn't* be seeing them." His voice was defensive.

She quickly changed the subject saying she would press his suit, unworn for over a year. "You'll need it for the funeral." It was a formal country.

Reluctantly he agreed. Together they told the children about their grandfather's death. In the middle of the explanations he had to leave the room, tortured by the memory of the bitter quarreling at their last meeting only weeks earlier.

Sarah drove Steve to the airport, only a short distance from the university town. A little early for the flight, they sat in the car. Sarah put her hand on his cheek. "I'm really sorry. I know you had your differences, but Dan was a nice man and I know you loved him."

Steve shook off her hand and looked away. "I guess I gave him a bad time. We were always on different sides. Neither of us was willing to give in. I always thought I had plenty of time to hold off. I hoped someday we could reconcile our ideas. Now it's too late."

Sarah gave him a weak smile. "One day you'll have a chance, Steve."

"That's childish nonsense—MK stuff." MKs were what the children of missionaries were called: missionary kids. Steve had picked the term up from Sarah whose own parents had been medical missionaries in Costa Dora. It was her knowledge of Costa Dora that had brought them together while they were students at the university. Their friendship had started out with an argument, for Steve thought missionaries had no place in Costa Dora. He always insisted, "We ought to just leave those people alone."

"But you aren't leaving them alone," she would point out. "You want a revolution. That means violence and death. At least my parents are *saving* lives."

The State Department had made his reservations, and he saw with mixed feelings that he was to fly there in first class. The comfort would be welcome but he could not overcome his distaste for the elitism. He was wearing jeans and an old jacket and felt out of place with the men in business suits. He tried to ignore the flight attendant's constant offers of magazines, coffee, drinks, headphones, pillows, and blankets.

Steve stared resolutely out of the window to the sea. Cuba materialized and then the coast of Central America. He tried to formulate some comforting words for his mother but anything that came into his head was a cliché. Strangely he did not know if his mother believed in some sort of afterlife. He knew she often went to the Costa Doran churches but he never knew whether she was drawn by the pageantry or by something deeper. He tried to find his own belief and could discover only a general feeling that someone as good as his father could not just be reduced to dust. There had to be something more. Sarah would have found the appropriate chapter and verse in the Bible. She was bringing the children up in her own faith. Hours ago Steve had been touched when seven-year-old Tim had shyly said, "Tell Gram I said her name in my prayers last night." He wished now he had Sarah's faith to comfort him. Blankets and pillows and magazines and headphones were not enough.

* * *

When he walked into the residency and saw his mother's pale, ravaged face, all the words of commiseration Steve had so carefully formulated on the plane fell away and he silently took her in his arms. Rosa brought them tall glasses of iced tea, and then discreetly left them. Together they went over the details of the funeral. Of course, Jean mentioned, the country's president would be there. Steve swallowed a caustic comment. Jean said that there was little for them to do, the embassy was taking care of all the arrangements. Dan's death was to be as much a matter of protocol as his life. "When will you be coming back?" Steve asked. "You know Sarah and I would love to have you with us, and so would the children."

"That's kind, Steve, but I'm going to stay here. At least for awhile. I don't have the energy or the will to think of moving, and I feel closer to your father here. You know we were hoping to retire to the old capital, at least part of the year."

Steve saw his mother glance toward the closed door. In what was almost a whisper she said, "Steve, I have to tell you the truth. You have a right to know, but it has to remain a secret." Steve watched with growing dread as Jean walked over to a desk and unlocked a drawer. She handed him a watch and wallet, both of which he recognized as his father's.

"You can see it wasn't a robbery," she told him. "But because of the election, the State Department thinks it's best to let people think it was. I don't understand this, though." She put a lighter in Steve's hand. "This was with his things. He didn't smoke. Where do you suppose it could have come from?"

Steve dropped the lighter as though he had been holding a menacing scorpion. He could not look at his mother. He felt his whole body shake. His life shifted from its foundation. It would never be the same. Nothing would ever be the same. Quickly he got up and left the room, terrified that his mother might read his mind.

* * *

Jean watched Steve leave, slamming the door as he went. She was shaken. Of course Steve would be shocked at the thought of something as planned and brutal as an assassination. She admonished herself for telling him. The assassins were most likely from the guerrillas, for Dan had been supporting the president— unless the military had done it, hoping for a coup. But if Steve believed it was the guerrillas then he might feel guilty, thinking of how often he had taken their side.

* * *

The following day was the funeral with its sad journey to the old capital. Since Jean had told Steve that Dan's death was an assassination, Steve had avoided any opportunity to be alone with her. Jean was shaken at the depth of Steve's wretchedness. He wandered from room to room, smoked cigarettes endlessly, broke off conversations in the middle of a sentence, and rudely ignored friends who had come to pay their respects. And the night before he had gone out and not returned until early this morning. He had been unshaven, red-eyed, unsteady, like a soldier returning from a terrible battle. There had been no talking with him. Any attempt to reach him met with an angry silence.

When Jorgé arrived, Jean thought Steve would be pleased. She knew Jorgé had been in trouble with the authorities. Surely Steve would be happy to see him looking so well. Jorgé took Steve aside. Whatever he told Steve only added to Steve's anguish. Steve turned a deathly white and stalked from the room. An hour after the funeral he gave Jean a perfunctory kiss and left for the airport.

6

After Dan's death Jean stayed on in Costa Dora, moving from the country's modern capital to the old city that had been the capital long ago. It was a city of ruins and suited her mood. Beside the devastation of conquest, revolution, and wars, all wrought by man, the town had suffered over the centuries the ravages of nature: volcanic eruptions and punishing earthquakes. Wherever you walked in the old city you saw streets blocked by landfalls and tumbled churches and convents. There were houses whose walls had been torn away so that their rooms were open to the air like stage sets.

Yet it was a city of great charm. Looking through the wrought iron gates the passerby glimpsed gardens with brilliant flowers and splashing fountains. There were intimate restaurants with tables set under ancient trees. And there were the people of Costa Dora, of whom Jean had grown fond. Half the population had descended from the ancient Maya. Because as a people they had survived so much misery—earthquakes, volcanic eruptions, poverty, epidemics, repeated invasions, and persecutions—they possessed a formidable patience and dignity. After Dan died, Jean watched them, telling herself that they were an example of how all things might be endured, but she did not possess their stoicism.

Jean began to spend hours in the country's old dark churches with their weeping Virgins and crucified Christs. She sought out God in his place of business to argue with him, to accuse him, to attack him for what he had done to Dan and to her, to taunt Christ to come down from his cross and listen to *her* suffering.

She was never alone in the churches. Processions were constantly arriving from the small villages. Peasants would walk for miles carrying a statue of their patron saint decorated with balloons and ribbons. Celebratory fireworks to attract God's attention exploded on the steps of the churches. Inside the church, the floors were covered with the scattered petals of flowers, and the air was suffused with the smoke and the acrid scent of hundreds of candles. It seemed impossible to Jean that in all the confusion God would notice her. She was certain her silent entreaties would be lost in the clamor. After awhile Jean gave up, sure that she would never be freed from the misery and loss of Dan's death.

She passed her days clinging to the comfort of routine, taking afternoon tea in a pleasant garden with some of the wives in the diplomatic corps who kept weekend homes in the old city. The women were kindness itself after Dan's death, although under the circumstances her staying on undoubtedly made them uncomfortable. She had become an embarrassment, a constant reminder of the dangers that lay beneath the civilized surface of the country, dangers to which they and their families were daily exposed.

Jean asked herself why she remained in a country where there were so many reminders of Dan's violent death. The answer was that she had nothing else to do. She had always been the wife of the counsel, or as Dan progressed up the diplomatic ladder, the wife of the first secretary, or the ambassador's wife. That had been her whole existence. She did not know what else she could do. With Dan gone, her life seemed in limbo, but what was she waiting for? She didn't even have a place to go. She and Dan had not lived in the States since their marriage. Her brothers had retired to Sun Belt condominiums at the edge of a sea or a golf course, content to live in enclaves of people whose familiarity to themselves reassured them. She might have settled in the university city where Steve and Sarah held teaching positions, Steve in the Spanish department, Sarah in the department of archaeology. She would have been close to her grandchildren, ten-year-old Mia and seven-year-old Tim. Yet she could not imagine herself away from Costa Dora.

Rosa had come to the old capital with her, and it was Rosa who one afternoon announced, "Someone to see you, Señora." Rosa appeared awed by the unexpected guest and Jean, thinking from Rosa's demeanor that it must be a government official or someone from the embassy, was surprised by the guest's appearance.

The woman Rosa ushered in was an indeterminate age, somewhere between fifty and seventy. She was wearing a shapeless dress with a torn pocket and worn sandals. Her grayish brown hair was braided and wound round her head in an old-fashioned crown.

The woman's voice was brisk and matter of fact. "I hope I'm not bothering you. You can just tell me to go away if you like, my feelings won't be hurt." She appeared to be an American. For a moment Jean thought she was one of those confused and lost creatures who used to turn up for help at the embassy, people who had come to Costa Dora to leave an old life or start a new one, the eternal wanderers of the world in search of an illusive something they could never name. Nothing could have been farther from the truth.

"I'm Dr. Jansen, Ruth Jansen. I have a small clinic here. I'm sure you've never heard of it. I apologize for intruding, but Pastor

Brock and his wife wrote to me from the Philippines. They were concerned about you, and asked me to call on you. Of course some busybody bursting in on you may be the last thing you need."

Pastor Brock was Sarah's father. He and Emily Brock had been missionaries in Costa Dora. The embassy had little to do with the missionaries in the country, and Jean and Dan had not met the Brocks until Sarah and Steve's marriage. By then the Brocks had left Costa Dora for the States. Now they were in the Philippines. Jean recalled the Brocks mentioning Dr. Jansen and her clinic with reverent admiration. "We don't know how she does it," Emily Brock had said. "Minimal funding, little help, and fifteen-hour days."

Jean hastened to welcome her, intrigued by her guest. "You were so kind to come. You're not intruding in the least. Please sit down and let me get you something cold to drink." Jean summoned Rosa and asked for lemonade. When Rosa returned she had brought a small feast of sandwiches and cookies as well, eagerly offering them to Dr. Jansen. Jean had never seen Rosa so respectful to a guest. When Rosa bowed herself out of the room, Jean said, "It would seem that Rosa knows much more about you than I do. All I know is that the Brocks have the greatest admiration for you. Won't you tell me what you do?"

"It's very quickly told," she said. "My clinic offers medical services to those who could not otherwise afford them. But I haven't come to talk about myself. I came to find out if I could be of any help to you."

"That's very kind. As you can see my life is not a hard one. I'm comfortable with Rosa to care for me and friends nearby." Then for some reason Jean could not explain she blurted out, "The truth is, I live from minute to minute, amazed at the end of the day I have survived without Dan. And a little regretful."

Dr. Jansen covered Jean's hand with her own. "Thank you for being honest with me. I have days like that, too. For the most part, though, I don't have time for despair. It's a good thing, too, for seeing the misery I see, I would have lost heart a long time ago.

"Forgive me for intruding on you. I'd wanted to meet you for some time. Something told me we would get along. Now I must leave for the clinic. I have surgery this afternoon, but you might like to drop by one day and see what we do."

As she left Dr. Jansen scooped up the uneaten cookies on the silver plate beside her and wrapped them in a crumpled handkerchief she pulled from her purse. "I hope you don't mind," she said. "We have a young patient who lost a leg and needs cheering."

Before Jean could ask where the clinic was Dr. Jansen was out the door and hurrying toward her car which was so old it had a running board. Jean watched while the automobile coughed and trembled and finally shook its way down the driveway and disappeared. "I won't get involved," Jean told herself. "My own problems are enough."

But the next morning Jean asked Rosa, "Do you know where Dr. Jansen's clinic is?"

"Oh yes, Señora. Everyone knows. It is at the *oriente* side of the market. It is not hard to find. You will know it by the line of people."

I'll just have a look, Jean told herself. The morning was cool and pleasant. She decided against driving, knowing that parking on the narrow and convoluted streets near the market would be difficult. She made her way across the central park where people were lounging on the benches. Many were tourists evading the women and children who were attempting to sell carvings and lengths of woven cloth to them. The park which had once been used for public hangings was now green with trees and bright with flowers. Jean walked along the cobblestone streets passing the expensive stores in the tourist section of the city. The windows held displays of jade and gold jewelry, fashionable clothing, paintings, and antiques. Scattered among the stores were cafés and more formal restaurants. Over the years she had been in all the shops. She and Dan had dined in most of the cafés and restaurants. Those things had once given her pleasure. Now they were merely part of a deadly routine.

As she drew closer to the marketplace the tourists were left behind and she found herself surrounded by Costa Dorans. The men were in white shirts and dark trousers; the women in gaily embroidered blouses and skirts, their hair woven into long braids. There was an elegance to the women's walk and many of them balanced baskets on their heads. Others shepherded their children ahead of them or wore a shawl tied over one shoulder to hold a baby. The shawls were woven in crayon colors and even the babies wore embroidered caps and jackets, so everywhere you looked there was a feeling of festivity. Yet these were their everyday clothes, and many of the clothes, Jean knew, were handed down from mother to daughter and mended and refashioned to preserve the cunning embroidery.

The marketplace itself was a feast of color. One stall had a display of hanks of embroidery thread in every shade of orange and green and yellow and blue. In another stall quilts were hung, each patch like a small abstract painting. Vegetables and fruits were arranged in pyramids of kaleidoscopic color. It had been years since Jean had been in the market, for Rosa did the shopping.

Jean suddenly regretted missing the liveliness of the market all those years.

In spite of the crowds there was no jostling, for the Cosa Dorans are the most diffident and polite of people. As she reached the east side of the market Jean saw across the *calle* a line of people in front of a small, dilapidated building. As she approached it she read a crudely lettered sign that said, "Clinic." She squeezed past the line. As she entered the building, she was taken aback by the odor of medicines, soap, and the unmistakable smell of sickness and poverty. One room held several cots, all occupied. Gathered around the patients or clustered nearby were the patients' families including several small children who were wandering about the room, running back and forth amongst the cots. Jean knew from visits to the hospitals in Costa Dora that hospitalization was considered a time of reunion for families. They could not imagine leaving even for a moment someone who was ill.

She was suddenly conscious of her appearance. Her gold bracelets and expensive clothes made her feel like she was eating a large meal in front of starving people. She was aware of how isolated she had been all these years from the people of Costa Dora. Apart from Jorgé, Rosa, Manuel, and the other servants at the residency, the only Costa Dorans she could call friends were the wealthy businesspeople and powerful politicians who frequented the embassy.

Dr. Jansen appeared unsurprised to see Jean. "Mrs. Pierce. Good morning. As soon as I'm free I'll show you our modest facilities." She smiled at Jean. "While you're waiting you might round up those children and take them off somewhere where they won't disturb the patients." A moment later the doctor had disappeared into another room.

Jean looked distractedly about. Finally she mustered the courage to call, *"Atención."* When that did not work she went among the cots and gathered the children up holding onto their jackets and skirts and shepherded them out onto a kind of veranda on the back of the clinic. There were seven children all under six or seven staring at her with wide dark eyes. Desperately she tried to think of something to keep their attention. *"Quieta!"* she said. "And I will tell you the story of the *tres pocos cerdos.*" She launched into in improvised version of the "Three Little Pigs." The children appeared entranced. They moved closer to her and were begging to try on her bracelets and fingering the silk of her dress. They asked for more stories. Encouraged, she tried "Jack the Giant Killer" and "Little Red Riding Hood." It was only when the children demanded to know every last thing in Red Riding Hood's basket of goodies that Jean noticed how thin they were. *"Mañana,"* she said, "I'll bring you a basket."

In the early afternoon Dr. Jansen swept Jean away on a tour of the clinic. "Two rooms for the sick patients," she said, "the dispensary, my consulting room, and the chapel. Once a week a Lutheran pastor comes to give a service for anyone who wishes to attend. The clinic is not very grand, I'm afraid. I hope you'll visit us again, Mrs. Pierce. You were a great hit with the children, and our patients were able to get a little much-needed rest."

After that Jean appeared regularly at the clinic carrying a basket of food. Often she stopped first at the market for flowers which she arranged in the chapel. She had noticed how many of the patients' relatives spent time in the chapel and she thought the flowers might cheer them. She spent more and more time with the children, too. But it was not only stories now but lessons in reading and writing, for Jean had discovered most of the children didn't attend school. What she longed to do was give the children a good bath and shampoo. Her second week at the clinic she discovered she had caught head lice and had to send a scandalized Rosa out for a special soap.

On some days there were deaths, and the sadness affected the whole clinic. Once Jean asked Dr. Jansen, "I can guess what you say to comfort the families, but what do you say to yourself? How do you account for all this suffering and poverty and death around you?"

Dr. Jansen shrugged. "I argue with God. I point out to him that a little more medicine or a better diet or less ignorance would have saved a life. I chatter to him all of the time. I ask him where he was when last week Matéo, a father of six young children, died."

"And what does he say?" Jean asked, thinking of her own angry defiance at God for Dan's death.

"He tells me he has his own plans and can't always humor me. But it is a question of which of us is the most stubborn. It is nothing to wrestle like Jacob with an angel. I go right to the top. Don't you have these arguments?"

"Yes. I was furious with God when Dan died. He was a martyr for his beliefs."

"Surely a blessed death."

Jean said angrily, "That seems smug."

"To die for one's beliefs? That kind of meaningful death is rare. By the way, I have noticed the flowers you leave each morning in the chapel."

"I'm sorry I spend so little time there."

Dr. Jansen gave her a sharp look. "Nonsense. You are there all day. I've often heard God exclaim over your flowers—through those of us who are cheered by them. You are making a difference here in many ways."

As Jean thought about it, it seemed true. That was why she felt the satisfaction at placing the flowers there, and why she returned day after day to the clinic and the children, and why for the first time since Dan died she was able to sleep at night. A kind of peace crept into her life. Now she was seeing how different her life might have been, how much she had left undone. The horror of Dan's death was still there but something else remained—a connection with the people around her.

She began to worry less for herself and more for Steve, for shortly after Dan's funeral she had received a letter from him saying that he had left his position at the university and was taking Sarah and the children to northern Michigan. He hinted that he was going to be writing a book and she tried to comfort herself with that hope. But the comfort was hard to sustain as the year passed with no mention of the book. Sarah's letters were clumsy and dissembling, letters full of frustration at having lost her hard-won position in the university's archaeology department. When Jean, increasingly worried, offered to fly to the States to visit, Steve had put her off, leaving no doubt that she was not wanted. Guiltily Jean told herself that she ought to have moved to the university town, that her presence there might somehow have prevented Steve from abandoning everything. But knowing how meager an influence one person has on another, she did not really believe it.

It was not a complete surprise, then, when Sarah's desperate call came. Even with the poor connection caused by Costa Dora's inadequate phone service Jean could hear the strain in her daughter-in-law's voice. Sarah spoke rapidly, like a child blurting out a long-nourished grievance.

"Jean, I want you to understand what I'm doing. I know you're not the kind of person to blame someone. And anyhow, it isn't Steve's fault. I know there's something bothering him—it isn't just his father's death; there's something else, something he won't talk about. But I didn't marry him to go off and live in the middle of nowhere. Jean, our pipes froze last winter. We had to get our water from a neighbor who lives a mile away. Sometimes it was so cold, we couldn't even undress at night. I can't face another winter like that.

"There's absolutely no one to talk to here. I'm completely out of touch with what's going on in my field. What's worse, I'm starting not to care. I didn't want to tell you in my letters, but Steve is working for the county road commission. We've been here over a year and he hasn't even unpacked his books."

Jean tried to find her way into Sarah's flood of words. "I had no idea. What can I do, Sarah?"

"The thing is, I've been offered a chance to go to Costa Dora to work on a Mayan dig with a group of archaeologists. I have to be there September fifth. Jean, I've got to go. It's my field of expertise and I know the country. I've got to get away from here and get some perspective. If I don't, I'm just going to take the children and leave Steve for good. I'm asking if you could come and stay with Tim and Mia. Steve says he can manage with a woman here who baby-sits for us, but I don't trust her with the children. She lets them run wild and laughs when they cheat at cards. The one evening we used her, she got them up to watch a really sleazy horror movie on late TV with her so she wouldn't be afraid."

Mistaking Jean's bafflement for hesitation Sarah added, "Jean, they're really nice children, and I'll make lists." Between women, the promise of lists was the ultimate reassurance.

Before she left town, Jean drove her car to the clinic. "I don't know when I'll be back, Dr. Jansen—weeks, months, years? I can't tell, but I have a feeling my life here is over. Anyhow, I want you to have my car. Think of me when you have those arguments with God. Remind him of me."

7

As Sarah headed for Costa Dora, Jean left it, not only for Sarah and for the grandchildren but for Steve as well. All those years Dan's work had kept them in countries where Steve, growing up, could not walk freely through the streets or speak his own language. Was that behind what was happening now? She had been so caught up in her own sorrow over Dan's death she had not given much thought to what it might mean to Steve to have his father murdered. She would do anything to make amends to Steve but she worried that he did not want her.

After a tearful parting with Rosa, Jean flew from Costa Dora to Miami and then to Detroit. After an overnight stay she set off with a rented car and Sarah's map. Having so recently left behind hot sun, snow-capped volcanoes, and every shade of green, there was little to cheer her in the flat, northern Michigan countryside with its empty fields and dark woods. The September landscape of dusty leaves and brown grass was depressing. The towns seemed deserted and without amenities.

Now, after four hours of driving she was only a few miles from Steve's house. Jean wondered if she would find her son a stranger. She dreaded the imminent meeting; it was Sarah and not Steve who had asked her to come and she worried that he would not welcome her. She felt certain that he would be on the defensive, as people who make grand gestures must be, for how can they know whether they have made a bold leap ahead or simply avoided what must still be faced?

The landscape around her suggested desertions. Silver-gray farmhouses stood with their windows boarded—or worse, gaping. There were abandoned orchards of crippled apple trees. Sandy slopes and fields strewn with stones told why the farmers had moved on. It was only early fall, but she could imagine what this country must be like when the snow fell. Sarah in a letter about the country had said it reminded her of the verse from Job: He hath stretched out the north over the empty place.

She understood why this cold north was so alien to Sarah, who had spent her childhood in the warm, sunny places of the world where her father, a doctor, and her mother, a nurse, had been missionaries. They were far away in the Philippines in a post they could not easily leave. It was another reason she had responded to Sarah's plea. Who else did Sarah have?

Once across the bridge, familiar from Sarah's description in her letter, Jean came to a crossing and turned onto the road whose name she recognized from the return address on Sarah and Steve's letters. A small boy was at the roadside, blacking out a name on the side of a mailbox. At the sound of Jean's car, he dropped his brush and disappeared into the woods. She looked at the partially obscured name on the box: Pierce. Her name. Steve's name. The child's name. The slash of black paint that nearly obliterated the name was like a slap in the face.

How old was Tim? Jean knew it was her grandson who had been painting out their name. Was Tim six? No, seven now. She was unprepared for the rush of feeling. He looked like Steve at that age, a darting long-legged water bird of a boy, with quick bright eyes and a crest of sun-bleached hair. She had not seen Tim and her ten-year-old granddaughter, Mia, since Dan's last leave nearly five years ago when they visited Steve and Sarah at the university. She and Dan had not been traditional grandparents. They were always thousands of miles away. Communication was through exotic gifts on their part and carefully lettered thank-you notes on the part of the children.

Jean turned onto a sandy driveway that led to a small cabin. Sarah had told her it had been someone's hunting shack, but even so, Jean was unprepared for its small size and its crudeness. Surrounding the cabin was a forbidding woods. An old truck that was missing a fender and much of its paint was parked beside the cabin. Jean's courage failed her. What had her son who once had been so full of promise come to?

Jean climbed out of the car feeling every one of her fifty-seven years. Her legs were stiff and cramped after the long drive, the feel of ground under her feet surprising. She was too uncertain of her welcome to bring in her suitcase. She prayed, *Let the door of the cabin open in welcome,* but nothing happened, which gave her the frightening feeling that God had remained in the clinic chapel and she was here on her own. Would she have to knock on the door like a stranger? That seemed inappropriate. Surely Steve would have been looking for her? Or heard her car?

As she approached the wooden screen door she was startled to see Steve standing silently behind it. She hardly recognized him. He was only thirty-five but he looked an old man. She had expected that living in the country and working on a road crew he would be fit and healthy. He was tanned, but too thin. He stared out at her through the screen like a prisoner about to receive an unwelcome visitor.

He was so still she was afraid for a moment he was not going to let her in. What would she do then? Would there be an angry scene? Would he turn her away? The screen door swung open.

"Hello, Mother. You found us." There was no welcome and no pleasure in his voice. "Sarah should never have asked you to come all this way. Sarah shouldn't have asked you. We could have managed."

For a moment Jean rested her hand on his bony, resistant shoulder. When she lifted her face he dutifully kissed her cheek. He had always been a polite child. "Can I bring in your things?"

At least, Jean thought, feeling reprieved, *he isn't going to send me away.* She had to find a way to reach this stranger. "Let's sit down for a minute first."

The interior of the cabin was unexpectedly attractive. Perhaps out of a desire to have civilized things around her in the wilderness, Sarah had set out her best bits of silver and china gleaned from the generous wedding presents the child of an ambassador would expect to receive. The adornments were a startling contrast to the rough log walls and the massive fireplace constructed of boulders like those Jean had seen shouldering up through the fields.

"Too much of the English gentleman in the jungle," Steve said, seeing her surprise in the room's attractiveness, "but Sarah seems to need it this way. While we're on the subject of Englishmen, I can offer you some tea. Nothing fancy, just the brand from the local supermarket."

She had been there only minutes and Steve was already looking for ways to escape. "I'll make it," Jean said, moving toward the small kitchen that opened off the living area. She was there to be helpful. She had no other excuse.

Steve brushed her help aside. "No trouble, although I expect you could do it in a pinch." She found some faint encouragement in this teasing reference to her legendary clumsiness in the kitchen. In the countries where they had lived, there had always been cooks among the servants.

Jean sat down in the living room. It was her plan to be frank with Steve. There were already too many unknowns. She called to Steve in the kitchen, "I saw Tim as I drove in. He was painting out the name on the mailbox. I suppose he thought I would drive by, not knowing you were here." Steve carried in a single mug of tea. So he would not join her. Even in primitive societies welcome was celebrated by a communal sharing of food. She took a deep breath. "If you want me to go back, I will."

Steve's silence went on for interminable seconds. "Of course you must stay. At least for the time being. You mustn't mind Tim. The children don't know you. That's all."

His statement seemed a rebuke. "I couldn't bring myself to leave the old capital, Steve. I couldn't have settled down in the States. I wouldn't have known anyone. I would have been too dependent on you and Sarah."

"I don't see how you could stay in the country where Dad was killed." Hearing the strangled sound of her son's voice, Jean could not look at his face.

"That's a ridiculous statement!" She tried to control her voice. She knew he had a right to be bitter about what had happened, but not toward her and not toward the country where it happened, a country she loved. "They were guerrillas, terrorists. They had nothing to do with the gov ..." She stopped and bit her lip, remembering that Steve had supported the guerrillas.

In an angry voice Steve said, "Of course it had something to do with the government. If you have a government that is a police state and an army of murderers, you will have terrorists."

"The government has to keep order."

"To *impose* it." He strode over to the window, his back to her, and stared out.

"Where would you not find violence of some sort?" Jean pleaded. "There were murders in your university town—a town that is supposed to be civilized."

"Exactly. That's why I left. I'm finished with cities. I don't want my children living there."

"But don't you miss the libraries, the theater, music?" She named what had been Steve's fondest pleasures.

"No." He swung around and stared angrily at her.

The resentment in his voice frightened her. Was he really prepared to give up on civilization? She tried a different tack. "You've already *had* all those things. The children haven't." Suddenly she stopped, afraid of the urgency in her voice and the anger in her son's face. "Steve, I'm sorry. I've only just got here. I didn't mean to start an argument."

She tried to change the subject. "Jorgé stopped by shortly before I left. He says to say hello to you. He seems to be working in some import–export business. He was wearing a business suit. I hardly recognized him. Manuel is very pleased."

Shortly before Dan had been killed, Jorgé had gotten into some political trouble. Days went by and nothing more was heard of Jorgé. Manuel looked glum and worried. He had had long conversations with Dan. When Jean had asked Dan about the rumor, Dan had told her it was nothing serious. Then Jorgé had appeared at Dan's funeral. It was only from the wife of someone connected with the army that Jean had learned what had really happened. Dan had risked criticism for interfering in local affairs to plead Jorgé's case with the government. Now Jorgé was safe and appeared to be on his way to becoming a businessman.

Oddly, Steve did not seemed cheered by her mention of Jorgé. Instead it made him even more withdrawn. She tried again. Forcing a smile, she said, "Tell me about your job. It seems very Roman, building roads." It was a weak attempt at humor.

"We don't build roads. Our work is more mundane. This time of year we clear trees and foliage from the roadsides. Spray them with defoliant." He gave her a wry look. "In other words spread a little poison, a perfect job for me." The irony must have seemed too heavy-handed, even for him, for he hurried on. "We scrape the gravel roads and put something on them to keep down the dust." For the first time since she had come Steve smiled. "You're sure you want to hear all this?" he asked. Yet he seemed as relieved as she was to have found a neutral subject.

Quickly she replied, "Being out of doors all day agrees with you. You look fit." It was not true but she longed to say something encouraging. She wanted to ask if he missed his job at the university but something told her it was like so much else—a forbidden subject. Instead she asked after Mia. "Where is she? I've seen Tim. I'm sure Mia has changed since I've seen her."

"She's in her room. I'll get her." Steve got up quickly, welcoming, Jean saw, the opportunity to move away from her worried inspection.

It was several minutes before Mia followed Steve into the room. Mia had Sarah's dark hair. It fell in soft waves about her face, nearly obscuring her half-quizzical, half-hostile expression. She was barefoot and dressed as any ten-year-old left to choose her own clothes would be, in a wrinkled shirt and soiled cutoffs. A blue feather was tucked behind her ear.

Jean got up from her chair and began to move toward the child, but Mia instantly retreated. Jean sat down again. "I hope you and Tim and I will have good times together," she said, knowing it to be a fatuous remark.

Mia did not bother to reply.

"Go outside and find you brother, Mia," Steve said. "Tell him that in spite of his efforts, his grandmother found her way to our cabin."

Mia shot her father a killing look and slipped out of the door.

"I'll bring in your things," Steve said and Jean could see that he was ashamed of his children's behavior. "Tim's moved in with me. You'll have his room."

"No wonder he wanted to keep me from finding the cabin," Jean said. She tried to make a joke of it, but the screen door slammed shut on her sentence. *At least,* she thought, *I'm going to be allowed to stay.*

As she made her way to Tim's room Jean saw that the cabin was small. Her presence would be more intrusive than she had supposed. The room that was to be hers was just large enough for a single bed and a chest of drawers. On the chest was a turtle shell. There were the vertebrae of some large animal, a twig with a cocoon, a collection of stones—one of which was a fossil—a nearly empty bag of hard candies, and a little pyramid of dried apple cores. Jean was pleased to see that the weaving of bright jungle birds she had sent Tim from Costa Dora was pinned up over his bed. But perhaps Sarah had put it there to please her.

Steve brought in her luggage. "I'll get Tim to clear his things out."

"No, don't do that. I'll manage." She welcomed the thought of living among his small treasures. "I've been in smaller quarters than this. Remember the summer we were driving through Patagonia?" Dan had been a first secretary at the embassy in Buenos Aires. The three of them had taken a short vacation in the Argentinean countryside the summer of Steve's thirteenth birthday, just before he left for prep school in the States. She could see the dry stretches of Patagonia now with the purple shadows of the Andes in the west and the flocks of sheep moving across the treeless fields like white clouds. "Do you remember there was no hotel in the town? We slept in a farmhouse. I remember the smell of wild thyme coming through the window."

"That was the village where they shot the mayor the next week," Steve said. "Quite a coincidence."

She turned on him. "Your father had nothing to do with that. Our visit was unofficial—a vacation."

"He met with the mayor while we were there."

"He didn't *meet* with him. He simply *talked* to him. It was a courtesy visit." How could Steve have remembered? She and Dan had never mentioned the incident in his hearing, and the Argentinean papers had given it no more than a paragraph or two.

"I'll let you unpack while I go and see if I can find the kids," Steve said, and left her.

As Jean sank down on Tim's narrow bed she felt a lump under her and pulling back the covers found a stuffed raccoon. She smiled. Thinking of the children Jean considered how difficult it must have been for Sarah to leave them for three months. She must have been desperate. Now, Jean thought, I am here in this place from which Sarah could not wait to escape.

8

Steve hurried from the cabin, welcoming the anonymity of the woods. He was furious with himself for having attacked his mother. None of it had been her fault. She had given up her friends and her comfortable life in the old capital to live in this dilapidated shack and care for two children she hardly knew and who wished she wasn't there.

But everything about her being there seemed wrong. She was a constant reminder of what he had come here to forget. He had not thought he would be able to face her and had nearly run into the woods with Tim to escape. He kicked aside a branch that had fallen across the path wondering how he would get through another day, much less weeks.

Yet he knew for the children's sake it was important for her to be here. Tim and Mia resisted obeying him. Knowing how it provoked him, they found ways to spend more time than ever out of his sight. They lived like wood sprites, squirreling away their food and carrying it off to some secret place. *They know something is wrong with me*, Steve thought. *Bitterness and desperation are catching.*

Steve had bought the run-down cabin because it came with forty acres of woods. Forty acres of empty woods seemed to offer all the isolation and protection he might need. At first he planned to restore the cabin, to replace, patch, shore up, and improve, but he found he had neither the skills nor the patience—nor, for that matter, the faith—and in the end the neglected cabin suited him. For a long time Sarah kept after him about repairs; then she stopped. Her resignation had bothered him more than the nagging. If Sarah, with her stubborn optimism, had given up on him, what could he expect of himself?

He resented being forced to look at the cabin through his mother's eyes. And he was furious with Sarah for summoning her. He knew Sarah had wanted her to come as much for him as for the children, though his mother was the last person he wanted to face.

With no sign of the children, Steve sat down on a mossy tree trunk, remembering it was here in the woods two days ago that he had first learned his mother was coming. He and Sarah had wandered outside with their after-dinner coffee and settled down on a bench in the yard. Evening was coming on, but there remained a half hour or so of light. It was a declining sun that didn't keep them warm. Steve had put an arm around Sarah's shoulder. Tim, wanting as much of his mother as possible before she left, sat on the grass, tickling her sandaled toes with a leaf. Mia had gathered an armful of knapweed, impatiently pulling them up by their loose taproots, and handed the prickly bouquet to Sarah. Sarah took it, lovingly brushing Mia's hair from her forehead with her other hand. Tim, wanting Sarah's hand on him, increased his tickling. Sarah laughed and reached down to tumble Tim over on his back and tickle his stomach. Mia joined in. *If it was me who was leaving,* Steve had thought bitterly, *the children would not care.*

Abruptly Sarah had straightened up. "You two go and see if you can find fresh deer tracks on the trail. I want to talk to your father."

The children had looked at Steve resentfully. He knew he had become little more to them than competition for Sarah's attention. He had lost the gift of giving them affection. Once it had been easy for him to show his love, teaching them checkers and chess, tumbling them on the floor, carving puppets, but children have short memories and are quick to sense weakness. Weak themselves, they are attracted to strength. But Steve needed all of his strength to fight his secret demons, the accusers that came by day and night to reproach and incriminate him.

As the children wandered off into the woods Steve felt himself stiffen. He did not know what Sarah had to say to him. And he had grown to expect bad news—but he had never dreamed of what she was about to tell him or he would have put a stop to it, which, of course, was why she had kept it from him. Their dinner had gone well. They each resolved to keep their last night together free from quarrels. Steve had already said everything he could think of to keep Sarah from leaving. "If you go to Costa Dora you'll be living in the country where my father was murdered," he said. "It's dangerous country."

"You only think that because of what happened to your father. Your mother lives there. I lived there for five years."

"Don't tell me there wasn't violence when you lived in Costa Dora. It wasn't only *my* father who was killed down there."

She could not deny it, for she had confided to Steve the story of her childhood friend, Maria, a Mayan whose father had been active in the union of agricultural workers. Government soldiers had come for him and taken him away. He was never seen again. Still, she was desperate to return to Costa Dora, to *escape* to Costa Dora. "But, Steve," she begged, "the university has had its digs there for years. Nothing has ever happened."

"But the digs are close to where the guerrillas have their camp."

"Thousands of tourists go to those digs every month, and nothing happens to them."

He saw that she had decided and he would not be able to find the words that would change her mind. If she weren't going to Costa Dora he might almost welcome her departure—or, rather, his isolation. It was not that he looked forward to being alone, for the thought of being thrown upon himself for company frightened him. It was rather that he was not fit company for anyone else. Otherwise, how could he let Sarah go? He would not allow himself to think what it would be like to sleep alone. He often awoke in the middle of the night, after dreaming of his father, and found he was huddled against Sarah's warm body, whimpering. Her arms would be around him and she would be wide awake. He would pull away, mumbling about a dream, and the next day he could hardly speak to her, frightened by his weakness and the depth of his need to confess everything, knowing with absolute certainty that she would leave him if he did.

He had been so involved with his own feelings that night, he had not paid attention to what Sarah was telling him until he was startled to hear her say, "I called Mrs. Crites and told her not to come." Sarah wore her dark hair in a long braid. When she was nervous, as she was that night, she nibbled at the end of it with her small white teeth.

Steve had no desire to have Mrs. Crites around. She smelled like decaying potatoes and made obtuse comments over the daily news: "If they're giving them cars away at those low prices, it's got to be because something's wrong with them." Her husband, Hazen Crites, considered he had hunting rights on their property and turned nasty when Steve, who would not allow guns so close to where the children played, and who, in fact, would not have guns on his property at all, turned him away. But there was no one but Mrs. Crites to care for the children. The plan had been for Mrs. Crites to be there when the children came home from school. Steve had to continue to work or there would be no money coming in.

"If you told Mrs. Crites not to come, who'll stay with the children?" he asked, with a wild hope that Sarah had changed her mind about leaving.

"Your mother. I called her and she's coming."

"Sarah!" He felt betrayed. "Why would you do that to me?"

"I didn't do it *to* you. I did it *for* you."

"You did it behind my back, as though I were a child."

"Running away is a child's trick."

When she was angry with him, Sarah told him truths about himself. It was unfair, and the only time he felt hatred for her.

Now that his mother had arrived, Steve tried to imagine whether it would be possible to spend four months in her company and decided it would not. He could not get up every day and face her. Sooner or later everything he was hiding would come out. Then she would hate him. As soon as he could bring himself to do it, he would tell her that she must leave. But first he would let her rest for a day or two.

He found her as elegant as ever. Wherever they were posted, she unerringly managed to find the cleverest dressmaker, the smartest hairstylist, the newest boutiques, but he noticed that the fashionable suit in which she arrived was a trifle too large. She had lost weight and she was pale. How could he bear these visible signs of her mourning? Was it his father's death or his own failure that was causing her anguish? Both, he supposed. It was a double reason for not wanting to have to see her.

She had come to do her duty, as she always had. He had seen her settling them into a new home in a new country, expertly directing movers in their own tongue, coping with ancient plumbing and inept servants. She gave her days away endlessly, entertaining visiting businessmen and their wives, carrying on the thousand tedious details of embassy life.

Steve's earliest memory was of his mother. They had been living in Spain. His mother had been on her way to a reception and had come into his room to say good night. Her blond hair was pulled back severely into a knot that rested low on her neck. She wore a gray silk dress and pearls and smelled like the lilies of the valley she had planted in the shade under his window, flowers she had had someone send all the way from America. She was smiling but he had the impression that she was actually afraid of leaving him, for what reason he could not guess. The memory of that look of fear on her face stayed with him, creating feelings of vague apprehension throughout his childhood when he was away from her.

Steve tried to tell himself that whatever his feelings about his mother being there, he must behave rationally, gracefully. No one was more sensitive than she was. She would never stay where she was not wanted, and however amiable he might pretend to be, she would soon recognize his real feelings and decide on her own to leave. Steve abandoned his search for the children. They were in one of their secret places in the woods and would return. They always did. He turned back toward the cabin, his path darker than ever in the diminishing light of the late afternoon.

* * *

Mia had discovered that if you stood at the edge of the woods behind the cabin, and looked toward the northwest, a bit of light came through the trees. If you entered the woods and walked toward the light, the trees suddenly stopped and you came upon a grassy bowl. Tim and Mia were sitting at the rim of the bowl. Around the bowl's edge wild asters in several shades of pink and purple were in bloom. If she and Tim came early in the morning or after dinner and sat perfectly still, and if the wind was in their favor, carrying away their scent, they sometimes saw deer nibbling on the tall grass. Once they had sighted a bald eagle swooping over the bowl, the shadow of its wings covering nearly the whole of the clearing. Tim had once seen a picture in a book of an eagle with a lamb in its talons. Seeing the eagle he had run crying to Sarah, afraid the eagle would carry him away. Mia considered Tim a baby. She told herself she did not need her mother. Unlike Tim, she could get along perfectly well without her.

Happening by accident on the children's retreat, Sarah had explained to Tim and Mia that their lair had been formed by a glacier rolling down from the north, gouging out the land as it went. This frightened Tim. He wanted to know if there were other giant snowballs poised, ready to tumble down upon them. Mia knew Tim did not like the bowl but she cherished its privacy and, having discovered it, regarded it as much hers as her own room. It was here that she thought up her schemes and assigned to Tim the part he was to play in them. It was here also that she criticized his performance until Tim said he wouldn't go there anymore and had to be wheedled into accompanying her.

Now Mia hurried to accuse Tim, "You let her see you painting our name out." There were no other children nearby, and with no one but Tim to carry out her notions, Mia was in the position of a talented director saddled with an amateur performer.

"I didn't *let* her, she just did. How was I supposed to know she was going to drive by just then?"

"You should have done it when I told you."

"Anyhow, I don't think you should have made me do it. *I* don't care if she stays or not. You said she was mean and bossy, but she's nice. She sent me the jungle birds."

"You had to give your room to her."

"I'd just as soon be with Dad." With his mother gone Tim had been happy to have his father nearby. His presence was nearly as comforting as Tim's collection of stuffed animals.

"She'll be after us all the time. Mrs. Crites would have let us do what we want." At first Mia had been unhappy at the idea of her mother's leaving, but when she understood that she would then be the woman of the house, she had been excited. Mrs. Crites would have come and gone, but Mia was there all the time. Besides, Mrs. Crites spent most of the day watching television. Mia had also seen her drink from the vanilla bottle and go through her mother's dresser drawers. All this gave Mia a feeling of power over Mrs. Crites.

A gun went off nearby. "It's Mr. Crites," Mia said. "He's poaching rabbits again. Let's sneak up on him."

"I don't like guns. Anyhow I don't feel good. I don't like what Dad cooks."

"It's disgusting the way you separate everything out on your plate."

"It's the only way you can see what you're eating."

Mia headed toward the sound of the gun.

Not wanting to be left alone in the dark woods Tim reluctantly tagged along. "Why can't we go back to the cabin?"

"The longer we stay away from the cabin, the more she'll know we don't want her here. You don't have to come along if you don't want to." Mia knew Tim was afraid of going back by himself.

To show his independence Tim lagged behind, probing a decaying tree trunk and carefully prying away a piece of soft, iridescent, greenish-blue wood to take home with him. Mia knew Tim would be after her the moment she was out of sight. He was always trailing after her. The thing was, with their mother gone, Tim could hang on to her, but she had no one to hang on to.

When he caught up with her, Tim asked, "Will Mom be back?"

"Yes, she left her good perfume and her silk caftan. I saw you smelling the perfume. Anyhow, if she doesn't come back the perfume and the caftan will be mine."

* * *

Hazen Crites stopped to slap his beagle affectionately on the rump. Every part of the dog's agile body squirmed with delight at this unaccustomed affection. Suddenly the dog started to yelp and made little dashings into the woods and back. At first Crites thought the dog had picked up the scent of a rabbit, or maybe a raccoon; then he heard whispering and said to himself, "It's those snooping Pierce brats on my tail again." He considered the day the Pierces had moved in to have been the beginning of trouble. Before them, old Mr. Trinker had lived in the cabin. All Crites had to do was drop off a rabbit or two and a haunch of venison and Trinker didn't care how much Crites hunted on his property—or for that matter, whether he hunted in or out of season.

When his wife, Edna, started baby-sitting for the Pierces, Crites believed the connection would entitle him to the use of the woods. As a goodwill gesture he had even taken over a rabbit to the Pierces', all skinned and ready for the pot, but Pierce's wife acted as if it were a poisonous snake. Crites had labeled her one of those eco-nuts who think wild rabbits are the same as pet bunnies. Her husband had gone on and on: "Would you mind, Crites, not hunting on my property?" Pierce had asked. "The children play in the woods and, anyway, I don't like guns."

The Pierces were city people, Crites decided, with no idea what was in their woods. They let it all go to waste. Crites knew the open patches of meadow where the wild strawberries were and a place where there were so many blackberries you never had to leave the trail, but just picked as you walked along. And there were ruffed grouse there, too. He knew of a few places where in May he was sure to find morel mushrooms. He could sell them for eleven dollars a pound to Ray Hodges, who trucked them to expensive restaurants in the city or dried them to sell to food stores. Crites knew that if you were just smart enough you could get money out of any land.

He could hear the Pierce children sneaking around after him. They'd be sure to tell Pierce on him for being in their woods with a gun. Crites considered shooting over the children's heads. "Give them a good scare," he said half aloud, to test the idea and even went as far as to raise his rifle, dropping it after a moment. He had to stay on the good side of Pierce so he could work him around to letting him go deer hunting on his property.

The beagle suddenly sprinted into the woods after a rabbit, making a broad sweep and then working the rabbit in increasingly tight circles until it was flushed into the open, where Crites had a clear shot.

* * *

At the sight of Mr. Crites holding the limp, bloody rabbit Tim looked sicker than ever, but Mia forgave Mr. Crites. She secretly admired him for the way he knew the woods. Since they moved up here her mother had read to them from books about birds and animals but Mia had learned a lot more by trailing Mr. Crites around as he picked their berries, gathered their mushrooms, and slaughtered their rabbits and grouse. Had he been the least bit friendly toward her, Mia would have kept his intrusions onto their land a secret, but he refused to take any notice of her, which made her want to let him know he had no business there. She watched from the trees until he was gone and then she walked over to the bright-red spots that lay on a mulch of pine needles. Curiosity made her reach down and touch the rabbit's blood. She was just inspecting the red smear on her finger, dispassionately considering it, when she heard Tim behind her being sick. She turned and directed a look at him of mingled sympathy and impatience, aware that she had seen her mother look at her father in the same way.

9

Many of the Mayan temples had not yet been excavated and were still covered with grasses. In the damp autumn twilight they loomed up in the tropical forest like great green hairy beasts.

The others on the dig had taken the van back to the dormitories anxious for an icy Coke and a shower after the long hours of working in the humidity of the September rainy season. Sarah had chosen to walk back. With others around her all day long there was little time to do the thinking she needed. She prided herself on being a rational person and believed the answer to Steve's dismaying behavior was there to be discovered if only she could sort things out. If she didn't find the answer she might have to leave him and she could not bear to think of that.

So exotic a place was the tropical forest after her year in the chilly wasteland of the north that Sarah could not get used to it. Everywhere she walked she knew she was walking over ancient ground full of surprises. In a game of archaeological hide and seek they were there to discover the sprawling palaces and lofty temples concealed beneath the seductive earthen mounds.

Sarah watched a spider monkey swinging through the branches of a nearby ceiba tree. The ceiba trees were sacred to the Maya and were portrayed in their hieroglyphics as a cross. In the Sunday school taught by her mother and attended by several of the Mayan children in their Costa Doran village, her mother had used the symbol of the tree to teach the children about Jesus and his death on the cross. Sarah found herself longing for that earlier time when everything seemed so simple. She would have given anything to talk with her mother now, to confide in her, but her mother and father were thousands of miles away in the Philippines.

She had come here to keep from leaving Steve, which she surely would have done had she stayed on in the north. The haunted look on his face, his angry withdrawal from her and the children, the refusal to confide in her had all become too much. She couldn't find her way back to him.

It had started after Steve returned from his father's funeral. He was transformed from the rather serious but congenial man who was the star of the Spanish department and a devoted husband and father, to a bitter, withdrawn stranger who not only wouldn't answer her questions but didn't even seem to hear them. He pursued one self-destructive path after another, culminating in his sullen and peremptory announcement, "I resigned from the university today."

Startled, Sarah had asked, "You have a job offer and you haven't told me?"

Defensive, he answered, "No. I just decided to resign."

"But that doesn't make sense. You were headed for tenure. I know you've been working hard on your book. Couldn't you have taken a leave of absence until it was finished?"

"That's what Abrabanel asked. I told him I wasn't coming back."

"Why didn't you tell me first?"

"Because you would have said just what you are saying now and it wouldn't have made any difference."

Sarah was stung into a furious silence. Then one morning, with no explanation, Steve packed a duffel bag and drove north leaving Sarah and the children. A week later he returned with a proclamation. "I bought a cabin. In the woods. That's where I'm going."

"What do you mean *you're* going? What about me? What about my teaching job? What about the children?" Sarah felt as though Steve were running faster and faster from her until she could barely see him in the distance.

"You can do as you like." His voice broke and the bitterness left it. To Sarah it seemed the voice of a small boy who has backed himself into a corner from which he can't or won't escape. In a strangled voice he muttered, "Of course I hope you and the children will come."

Somewhere between fury and panic, Sarah cried out, "You can leave whenever you want to, and the sooner the better." Tim and Mia, awakened by the shouting, came down from their rooms and stood on the stairway, crying. Steve rushed by them, taking the stairs two at a time. Sarah could hear dresser drawers pulled open and slammed shut. He was taking her at her word. Suddenly she was more frightened than she had ever been. She clung to the children in the guise of comforting them. *For better or for worse, in sickness and in health. Surely,* Sarah had thought, *this is sickness.*

For the thousandth time she wished her parents were there so she could talk with them. She supposed they had spoiled her a little. They had been married for years and had given up hope for a child. When their prayers were answered and she had been born they had named her after the biblical Sarah who had waited so long for a child. She knew what they would advise: patience and prayer. In her circumstances, one thing harder than the other. She reached back to her childhood prayers, comforted by their direct simplicity. Quietly she put the children back to bed and went in to see Steve. "Wait a week, and if you still want to leave I'll go with you." It all seemed so bizarre she hoped a week's thought would make the difference, but at the end of the week Steve was more determined than ever.

Reluctantly she took a leave of absence from the archaeology department, found a renter for their small house, and began to tell the children exciting stories about pioneers and Indians who lived in the north woods as they were going to do. The one thing that sustained her was the hope that this was only a phase, an over-reaction to Dan's death.

But the months turned into a year. Their whole life was on hold. She was growing bitter and the bitterness was affecting the children. Mia was becoming quarrelsome and Tim had started having nightmares. Their family was in a lifeboat and the weight of Steve's misery was weighing them down. If Sarah didn't leave they would all drown.

Finally, just as she was giving up and preparing to take the children and leave Steve, this opportunity to work on the Mayan dig had turned up. They wanted to start new excavations in the fall. They wanted her expertise. The opportunity seemed heaven-sent. She could leave Steve without leaving him. And she could use these months to try to solve the puzzle, to discover what had happened to Steve, perhaps find a way to bring him back to life.

Just ahead were the dormitories for the archaeological team. They were jerry-built with rusting corrugated tin roofs weighed down with rocks. But the slight accommodations were welcome at the end of a long day. During the day the team worked under the hot sun, laboriously whisking away grains of dirt, uncovering the footings of a room or a shard of polychrome pottery, traveling backward in time one teaspoonful of dust at a time.

There was always an undercurrent of excitement, for they never knew what they might find or what it might mean. Sarah knew unlocking secrets of the past could be as exciting as any of today's technological advances. The digs unearthed a series of clues like a treasure hunt. Yesterday's discoveries had to be reevaluated in the light of today's discoveries. For instance, archaeologists had triumphantly proclaimed the finding of stone hand axes. Now, years later, it was thought that those "hand axes" had been nothing more than the useless pieces of stone remaining after chips of stone were chopped off and harvested for some unknown purpose. It was the chips that were wanted. For all the digging and studying, ancient civilizations were maddeningly elusive.

Some days they were lucky. That was what kept them going during all the dull and tedious labor. Yesterday had been a landmark, a once-in-a-lifetime find. They had uncovered the figure of a warrior. The first thing uncovered was a half inch of soft glitter. There were shouts of excitement, for it could be nothing but gold. Everyone at the dig gathered around. Working with surgical scalpels and small camel-hair brushes, grain of dust by grain of dust Dr. Reisner had delivered the warrior into the twentieth century.

The statue was no more than nine inches, yet it conveyed a feeling of authority and threat. The thousand-year old statue was carved from sandstone and embellished with jade eyes and gold earrings, a priceless find. The news had already reached the outside world. They had received congratulatory faxes and calls. The statue would go to Costa Dora's museum, but the credit would go to Dr. Reisner and his workers. Sarah smiled as she thought of the scholarly papers the discovery would generate. She might attempt one herself.

As she reached the dining room where the staff had begun to gather, Sarah could hear excited chatter. The triumphant archaeologists were reliving their discovery. As she walked into the room she found them gathering around the table for dinner. Seeing their excitement and Sarah tried to put aside her worries about Steve.

Dr. Reisner's face was flushed with pleasure, his hands moved expressively as he described in staccato exclamations the moment they had discovered the warrior. Reisner was a large bear of a man and his broad gestures nearly swept the dishes from the table. "Early post-classic, unquestionably," he said.

The statue itself was displayed in the center of the room propped up on a table. The warrior's expression showed no hesitation. No question of the battle's right or wrong appeared on his countenance. Sarah could not help thinking that it no longer mattered now if the soldier, whose image the statue was meant to mirror, had been buried after a victory or a defeat.

In the evening Sarah was entrusted with locking up the warrior. They had no safe but the little room where their more valuable finds were secured. It had a barred window and a locked door. Still, she worried, it would not have been difficult to break into the room. The lock was worn, the door cheap plywood, and the bars on the window rusted and loose. Alone in the room she held the warrior in her hands, recalling her courtship with Steve. In those days Steve had been like that warrior, certain of his ideas, eager to battle those he labeled the enemy.

She and Steve had been graduate students. Steve was spending the summer with his parents, writing his thesis on the indigenous literature of Costa Dora. Sarah had been in Costa Dora with a group of students working on Mayan ruins. She was glad to be back in the country where she had lived from the time she was

nine until her fourteenth year when her parents had been trans-
ferred to another Central American country at the government's
request. The government had evidently felt they were having too
much influence in the village. They had blamed her parents for
efforts in the village to inaugurate an agricultural union and for
talk of the need for better wages.

It had been her first dig and she found it hard work carving
away centuries of grass and trees to reveal a burial site or the great
stone steps of a temple. The ruins they were working on were
those of an ancient city where 200,000 people had once lived. The
soaring pyramids were built to represent the mountains, the great
plazas of the city to represent the sea.

The students had camped out in tents in the jungle under
mahogany and cedar trees. Howler and spider monkeys swung
through the treetops, and each night the students had to search
their campsites for snakes. They went to bed and woke up to the
cries of birds whose colorful feathers made Sarah feel the birds
had escaped from some exotic painting.

She and Steve had dated casually at the Michigan university
they both attended. They had met at a lecture on Costa Doran
poetry. When Steve heard she was working on a dig there he
invited her to spend a week with his family. During a lull in the dig
she flew to the old capital where the ambassador and his family
escaped the heat of the city for a few weeks each summer. After
the rigors of the tropical forest the Pierce home was a delight. It
was hidden behind tall walls with rooms that opened onto a court-
yard of flowers. Sarah and her parents had once visited the old
capital. They had stayed with a missionary family in their small
home. She remembered touring the city and looking with an envy
she couldn't repress at the handsome homes with their flowered

courtyards. She had never thought to be staying in one of those homes.

Sarah had found Dan to be an imposing, handsome man with a quiet, sardonic humor, and had been impressed with Jean's cool competency as a hostess as well as her knowledge of the Mayan culture and religion. When Jean engaged Sarah in a discussion of Mayan temples Sarah could not contain her surprise. "Mrs. Pierce, how did you ever learn so much about the Mayans?"

Jean had said almost timidly, "Oh, I've always been interested in religion."

Steve laughed and said dismissively, "Mother's never seen a church she didn't like." Sarah knew Steve was not comfortable in those churches. He complained to her that the pungent odor of incense sickened him, the business of people coming and going distracted him, and the peasants who knelt with bowed head and arms outstretched, reliving the crucifixion, made him uncomfortable. Now he said to his mother, "In this country the people don't need faith, they need a job and food."

Dan rebuked Steve. "Let your mother have her churches, Steve. With your penchant for trouble, this family needs all the prayers it can get."

Sarah had no idea what Dan had meant until Steve had asked to borrow Jean's car for a few days saying he wanted to drive Sarah back to the dig. Jean had given him a long look. She said, "It's a miserable road. Are you sure Sarah wouldn't be better off flying back?"

Steve had insisted. The next morning there was an early breakfast and Jean and Dan had seen them off. Jean was unusually quiet, Dan almost grim. When they were alone in the car Sarah asked, "They seemed worried. Is the road really that bad?"

"The road is a challenge, but it isn't that. They think I'm going to see the guerrillas. Their camp is only a half day's drive north of your dig. They're right. I'm going to take you there. Mother and Dad worry that someone in the government will hear that the son of the ambassador is playing footsie with the guerrillas, but I know how to be careful. No one is going to find out."

The guerrillas were a band of revolutionaries who were fighting the repressive regime of the country. In the many years of fighting there had been thousands of murders on both sides. Sarah knew too much about the conflict. In the Costa Doran village in which her father had his clinic there was constant warfare. She had been thirteen when government soldiers had come and carried off the father of her best friend, a Mayan girl, Maria. The father had been suspected of being sympathetic to the guerrillas when he actually had merely been trying to get something more than starvation wages for the people in the village who worked at a plantation picking coffee. The townspeople had been equally frightened of the guerrillas, for when the guerrillas were seen around a village the government soldiers punished the whole village. The idea of actually contacting the guerrillas alarmed Sarah. "But isn't that dangerous?" she asked Steve. "They would certainly be suspicious of a stranger."

"I'm not a stranger," Steve boasted. "I have a friend, Jorgé, who helped me make contact with them a couple of years ago. I convinced them I was on their side. They know of course that Dad is the ambassador, but they've forgiven me that."

"What do you mean, forgiven you? What is there to forgive?"

Steve scowled. "Sarah, our country has been supporting the very regime down here the guerrillas have been fighting. I mean, I think it's decent of them not to hold Dad's position against me."

"But Steve, it doesn't seem fair to your parents for you to be friendly to their enemies. I know the government has been accused of committing murders, but the guerrillas have been responsible for murders, too."

"Not nearly as many as the government's soldiers have. I know that if the guerrillas take over the government there will be some violence but eventually there will also be justice."

"You're saying the guerrillas are justified in their violence because they mean well."

"Sarah, that's the old argument that says means don't justify ends. That's for impotent philosophers to sit around and argue. This is the real world. You can't have a revolution without some upheaval."

"I know the old revolutionary argument that you can't have a revolution without breaking eggs, but we aren't talking about eggs, we're talking about human beings. I don't pretend to understand these things, Steve, and I'm not sure I want to, but 'upheaval' is a rather innocuous word for murder. I just think you ought to call things by their right name. I'm no apologist for the government. Their soldiers took away the father of my best friend. But the Maya in our village were almost as afraid of the guerrillas as they were, the government soldiers. Most of the guerrillas were part Spanish. The people in the village knew the guerrillas looked down on them because they were Maya. The guerrillas believed the Maya just got in the way of the revolution, that their beliefs and customs were some sort of a hindrance to their plans."

"You don't know anything about it."

"I know a lot. I lived for five years with the Maya in their own village. You've lived in a fancy residency. The only Maya you know are servants. The Maya were my friends."

After that they sat for several miles in angry silence until Steve put an arm around her, nearly causing the car to go off the road. "Look, I'm not asking you to take sides. Just get to know these men. Maybe you'll change your mind."

By the end of the trip Sarah was exhausted by the heat and the rough road and still apprehensive about their destination. Once they had stopped to change a tire, another time to fill the car's radiator with water Steve had brought along. They spent the night camping out on someone's farm where the rented sites included a shower. By now Steve was in high spirits like a child who has been promised a treat. After a short drive he stopped and pulled two shirts from his duffel, giving one to her and putting the other one on himself.

Sarah was reluctant. "But we're not guerrillas. They won't like our wearing their uniform."

Triumphantly Steve told her, "They gave me the shirts."

Sarah put the shirt over her T-shirt. It made her uncomfortable. "I feel as if I were playing at dress-up," she complained. She had heard stories about the guerrillas' violence. Of course the government was brutal as well, but she was not sure she wanted to be identified with the guerrillas. Still, this masquerade seemed to give Steve so much pleasure she did as she was asked.

As they wound through the jungle and up a narrow mountain road she found herself caught up in a spirit of adventure. *Perhaps,* she told herself, *we'll come to some Mayan ruin that hasn't been discovered,* and she stared from the car window into the jungle. But it wasn't a forsaken ruin that caught her eye. Just ahead of them a man stood at attention. Like them he was wearing camouflage and he had a machine gun pointed directly at them.

Sarah was terrified, but Steve jumped out of the car and

engaged the man in an animated conversation. The man took some sort of walkie-talkie from his pocket and, after what seemed an endless conversation, their car was allowed to pass, but by now Sarah had lost all interest in the expedition. "Steve, let's turn around and get out of here. They may never let us leave." She could see the headlines, "Two University Students Held Hostage in Central American Country."

"There's nothing to worry about. You don't think this is the first time I've been here? They know I'm their friend."

At the end of the road a dozen men stood waiting for them. They greeted Steve warmly and exclaimed less happily over Sarah. With amazement Sarah heard Steve tell them she was to be his wife. Although she loved Steve and believed he loved her, they had never talked of marriage. Steve grinned down at her.

"Convenido?" Agreed?

She grinned. *"Con mucho gusto."* With pleasure. Sarah decided Steve clearly needed someone to take care of him. Why shouldn't it be her?

They shared the guerrillas' dinner of fried plantains and *chuchitos*, corn dough stuffed with spiced meat and wrapped in a corn husk. Everyone ate greedily as though, Sarah thought with a shiver, it might be their last meal. The guerrillas seemed to accept Steve as a partisan. There was much slapping of backs and coarse jokes. Of course they knew Steve's Spanish was nearly perfect but she guessed they had no idea her own Spanish was as good, for she had had little to say and hadn't joined in the laughter over the jokes. That she spoke a Mayan language fluently would never have entered their minds. And she preferred to keep it that way. She had no desire to talk with these men.

Steve was included in all their conversation, which was low and rapid. Evidently they felt that by speaking rapidly she would not understand them. There were many suspicious looks her way. She tried not to listen but certain words carried: urgency, sacrifice, revenge. One of the men, Carlos, who appeared to be their leader, had seemed hostile to Steve. Sarah had caught him for one unguarded moment looking at Steve with hatred and contempt, but a second later he was smiling and joking with the rest.

Sarah had never forgotten that look. The next day when she and Steve were driving away from the camp she tried to tell Steve about her fears. "That's your imagination. Carlos and I are *camarados.*"

Now here she was back again in Costa Dora. So much had happened in her life since her trip with Steve to the guerrilla camp. She wanted to forget that whole episode, to think the guerrillas were far away from the dig, but that wasn't so. She wrote Steve long letters reassuring him that she was safe but she hadn't mentioned in her letters that a couple of the younger and more adventurous students had spent a Sunday driving through jungle trails and had come back saying they had seen men in camouflage carrying rifles. Dr. Reisner had shrugged off the story saying, "Guerrillas? I've heard a few of them have infiltrated the hills near here. There's nothing to worry about. There are soldiers everywhere. The guerrillas aren't going to start anything."

Now as she prepared to lock the Mayan warrior safely away she thought again of Carlos and the guerrillas and the government soldiers and all the deaths. She was not much given to irony but it seemed to her fitting that the warrior should have been discovered in a grave site. Carefully she placed the statue in the box that had been specially made for it. As she put the top on the box, she felt for a moment as though she were putting on a coffin lid. Suddenly she wished the warrior was once more hidden away forever in his burial ground.

10

Left to herself, Jean unpacked, placing her lipstick and perfume alongside Tim's turtle shell and apple cores. On the bedside table she made room for Dan's photograph among a collection of shells, many of which she recognized as shells she had gathered and sent to Tim.

Finally, exhausted from the trip and the emotional roller coaster of her arrival, she stretched out on Tim's bed. It was not unusual for her to lie down in the afternoon. It was the custom in the countries in which she had lived. Dan often took time off in the hottest part of the afternoon for a siesta. The two of them would lie side by side as the breeze came through the closed shutters. It was a feeling as solid and secure as the carved mahogany dresser that stood in the corner of their room, a piece of furniture that was undeniably oversized but had followed them from post to post like a part of the family. She could not rid herself of the idea that she must hold on to Daniel's image or he would escape her altogether. A hundred times a day she meticulously attempted to visualize his fading features. The memory of his face was becoming an uncompleted sketch. Soon, she feared she would be left with nothing but his photograph.

Jean heard the screen door slam and, thinking it might be the children returning, hurried out of the bedroom, as much to see them as to escape the memories that in the small room were growing to immense proportions.

Steve was standing alone in the living room. "I looked for Mia and Tim. I'm afraid they're off in the woods someplace." His voice was apologetic.

He sat down and she followed his example, careful to keep her distance, for her son seemed as skittish as some wary animal peering out of its hiding place in some dark forest.

"What do you hear from the university?" she asked, aware at once that the question was awkward. It was far too soon to allude to Steve's flight.

He had been gone from his teaching job at the university for only a year, but Steve's face took on a blank, abstracted look as if he could not recall where the university was or even what it was. "I don't hear much, really," he finally said.

She persisted. "Dr. Abrabanel?" Abrabanel was her best hope; he was an old friend of Dan's and hers from Madrid who had taken a position at the university. In time he had become Steve's mentor.

"I'm afraid he's given up on me."

Sarah had once told Jean that Abrabanel was grooming Steve to take over his job one day as chairman of the Spanish Department. Steve spoke Spanish as well as he spoke English. His nannies had all spoken Spanish. It was the first language he had learned. When he was older he had met at embassy parties many of the poets and novelists whose work he had later taught to his students. Although, as he often angrily reminded his father, some of the best writers had disappeared—the lucky ones into jails.

Steve asked Jean a few polite questions about embassy personnel he remembered from his visits or had heard of in her letters. She saw he was making an effort to be pleasant, and began to relax. Perhaps he had not minded her coming as much as she believed, or perhaps he was getting used to the idea of her being there. She even began to imagine that this might be a pleasant stay. She would have a meal ready for him as she always had had for Dan, although, she had to admit, it was never a meal she had cooked herself.

She envisioned comfortable nights ahead in front of the fireplace. Steve would have amusing stories about the men on the road crew with whom he worked. The children would chat about their day at school. Little by little she would find ways of showing Steve how he was wasting his life here in this desolate place, a place she could not imagine choosing as a place to spend her life. She would encourage Steve to return to the university so that he and Sarah could take up their real lives.

Thinking of her daughter-in-law she said, "I'm sure Sarah has missed the university. It's wonderful that she has this opportunity. I told her that if she needs a little R and R down there I have friends in the city who will give her a weekend away from the digs: a room for herself, a hot shower, and a good meal. I don't suppose the archaeological team is living in luxury." Hesitantly she asked a question that had been on her mind, "I suppose ... the university digs are perfectly safe?"

She was totally unprepared for Steve's furious look. She couldn't imagine what she might have said to anger him so. He rose abruptly.

"I'll get our dinner started," he said in a barely controlled voice.

She wanted to follow him into the kitchen and ask what was wrong, but she was afraid of his rage. The room was growing dark but she did not know if she should turn on a lamp. How was she to move among the uncharted paths of Steve's wrath? She sat looking out at the woods, which seemed to be playing a children's game of moving closer to the cabin when she was not looking.

The sound of a motor startled her; civilization seemed far away. She heard a car door slam and walked over to the window. A man was helping Tim and Mia out of a pickup. He had grizzled gray hair, a red beard, and a solid, unyielding look to him as though he had grown like a sturdy tree from the ground. He walked up the path with all the confidence in the world in the earth's firmness.

* * *

Harry Wachner had come upon the Pierce children on the way to his own cabin a mile from the Pierce home. Mia was shepherding along a crying Tim. When Harry stopped to offer them a ride he saw at once that Tim was ill.

Harry was the Pierces' closest neighbor. He owned a small newspaper in which he published observations on nature, tips on hunting and fishing, and assaults on anyone who tampered with the river that ran through the county. He supported his newspaper by acting as a guide for sportsmen who came up from the city in the summer to fish the river, which was thought by many—Harry included—to be one of the finest trout streams in the Midwest.

While Harry was a man who minded his own business—as a guide he was amicable but reserved—he was always ready to lend a helping hand. He had called on the Pierces when they first moved in. His intention was to let them know he would be glad to give any help they needed in settling in and then to back off, leaving them to decide if they wanted to see more of him.

His plan changed the first time he looked at Sarah and Steve.

For two young people who seemed to have it all—intelligence, looks, education, two attractive children—they were clearly miserable. He had seen many young couples, anxious for a simpler life, leave the city in order to live and to raise their children closer to nature. But it was clear Sarah and Steve were different. They were running away *from*, not coming *to* something. He added them to his list of God's creatures needing his care, rather like the fawn he had bottle fed until it could be on its own and the trio of young owls he had rescued from a nest in a fallen tree and was presently nurturing along.

It had not been difficult to keep an eye on the Pierces, for Tim and Mia often wandered down to his home to watch him repair snowshoes or tie flies for trout fishing. Steve came to ask for advice from Harry about a leaking roof and a stubborn water heater. Once Sarah had run over to his cabin pulling the children with her, afraid the furnace was going to blow up. Watching Steve and Sarah struggle with the normal problems of a homeowner had confirmed Harry's feeling that a course in "real life" ought to be required of all academics.

Once or twice Harry felt Steve was curbing an impulse to confide in him, but Harry was not one to push his way into someone's life and at the last moment Steve had changed the subject. Sarah was more forthcoming. "The truth is, Harry, that I hate this place," she had once confided in him when Steve was not there. "I feel buried alive and all my training is going to waste."

She had brightened a little when he told her about a secret Indian burial ground he had discovered. He had been looking for a large boulder to use in his garden. When he found several such boulders in the woods, one just the size he wanted, he had begun digging, planning to put a chain around it and winch it up onto his truck. The rock had been nearly excavated when a skull was uncovered. He had been shocked, thinking murder, but a few minutes later he had discovered a pipe bowl of stone and then a knife. He had reported his find to a local Indian chief who had indicated that the other boulders marked graves. The chief had sprinkled tobacco over the ground to reconsecrate the burial site. Sarah had been fascinated with the story and had begged Harry to take her to the site. There she displayed what Harry considered the proper amount of reverence, recounting stories to him of bones she had discovered in archaeological digs and how much in awe of them she had been. After that they had become good friends and he had kept his eye on the children. So when he saw that Tim was ill he had immediately put them into his pickup and brought them home.

As he shepherded the children into the Pierce home he looked with interest at Steve's mother. He thought Jean stylish though too pale. Like her son she appeared to be struggling with her own private worries, giving life only half her attention. Then he remembered that her husband had been murdered in a distant country and he reproached himself for judging her.

Steve shepherded the children into the house. Turning to Harry he said, "Come in and let me introduce you to my mother."

"Very nice to meet you," Harry said. "I found the kids on the road and figured they were late for dinner, so I gave them a lift."

"We saw Mr. Crites," Mia said to Steve. "He had his dog and we saw him shoot a rabbit right on our land after you told him not to."

Steve's voice was angry. "What's the matter with that man? I've told him not to hunt here."

Harry regarded Steve. Steve was talking about Crites, but Harry was sure Steve's quarrel was with someone else. He tried to temper Steve's anger. "Crites has been hunting on this property most of his life. I guess he figures that gives him certain privileges."

Steve bristled. "I suppose I have a right to keep anyone I like off my property." Steve turned to the children. "Mia, you and Tim had no business getting that close to anyone with a gun. If you see him again, you're to come directly to me."

Harry tried to change the subject. "Steve, your boy might be a little under the weather. He seems to have a touch of something. The plain fact is he threw up in the pickup." Harry caught a killing look from Mia. Evidently the girl didn't want her father or her grandmother to know about Tim's illness.

I suppose I'm interfering again, Harry thought. He was anxious to get away. The Pierces were people who did not seem to be able to get hold of their lives. As a guide Harry was exposed to more than he wanted of people like that. Handling the canoe, making a suggestion or two as to where a cast might be aimed, he often listened while men from the city, yearning to be purged and purified by the river, rambled on in what was half conversation, half confession.

They spoke of their wives, their children, and missed opportunities, of things they had done or resisted doing to keep their businesses and lives going. He would sit silently in the back of the canoe, listening like a priest in the confessional, in turns sympathetic, saddened, and appalled. Steve Pierce was like those fishermen. He was a man who had come north looking for some sort of peace from the land—but who had no intention of giving anything back.

Now he stood up and made his excuses to leave. "Nice to have met you, Mrs. Pierce." Before she could turn her face away he was startled to see tears in the woman's eyes. He hurried from the house as from some scene of despair and doom.

*   *   *

After Harry Wachner left, Mia saw Jean looking worriedly at Tim. Mia was furious with Tim for throwing up. When he was sick in the woods she had warned him that if their grandmother saw that he was ill, she would stay on.

Mia knew now that she had been right. Their grandmother dropped to her knees beside Tim and was holding her hand to his forehead. The other hand was smoothing back Tim's hair. Mia saw with disgust that Tim appeared to enjoy it.

Even worse was the expression on her father's face. She hated it when he worried so over them. It turned everything around and you ended up worrying over him, which wasn't the way it was supposed to be.

11

Jean watched the doctor climb from his pickup truck and head toward the house. The doctor, Len Brady, was Steve's age, tall and angular with a harried look as though he was always playing catch-up. "Sorry to turn up such a mess," Brady apologized. "I was putting a wood stove in our house."

Although he scrubbed his hands, narrow crescents of dirt remained under his nails. Jean was taken aback thinking of the soft-spoken, Spanish doctors in the countries where she had lived, doctors with dark suits and pale, well-groomed, immaculate hands, who made a little formal bow to a patient before they began their examination. She had preferred them to the American doctor at the embassy. The Spanish doctors' solemn, wary approach to illness, their very reluctance to offer reassurance, made you feel better.

While Dr. Brady percussed Tim's chest he chattered on about the advantages of one stove over another. "Touch of flu," he said at last. He left a prescription for an antibiotic and promised Tim would be up and around in no time.

But the week went by and Tim kept to his bed, eating little and tossing restlessly in his sleep. Several times a night he climbed out of bed and wandered half-sleepwalking into Jean's room to be comforted.

"He misses Sarah," Jean said.

Steve shook his head. "Yes, but I think it's more than that." He smiled at Jean. "I think he wants to be sure his grandmother stays on. He knows as long as he's sick you won't leave. After all, what would Sarah say if she knew one of the children was ill and there was only Mrs. Crites to watch over him? You will stay, won't you?"

"Tim" wants me to stay, Jean thought, *not "we" want you to stay.* Still, it was a relief to be wanted by someone. "Of course," she replied.

That night Jean overheard Steve assuring Tim that his grandmother had promised to stay on until Sarah returned. The next morning Tim's fever was gone.

Gradually things began to improve. Jean learned to avoid the topics Steve did not want to talk about: Sarah's absence, the university, Spanish literature, the world, his future. There were still a few safe topics: Tim getting better; the changing season; and her tentative explorations of what lay outside the door, which she tried to make amusing by casting herself in the role of a fool. It was not hard for her to do, for she was forever bringing in "unusual" leaves and plants or describing "exotic" birds, all of which proved commonplace to everyone else. Mia was scornful of Jean's ignorance, adding to the answers she gave to Jean's questions, "Everyone knows that."

And then she met the owls. Jean had just returned from a grocery shopping expedition to the nearby town. There she had been gratified to find the checker at the small supermarket recognized her from an earlier trip. The checker's friendliness added to Jean's small hoard of feelings of belonging. She was struggling to carry grocery bags into the cabin when three owls sifted down from a tree and flapped about the grocery bag. She ran into the cabin breathless and exalted, believing she had had a boreal visitation that at once flattered and terrified her.

Mia dismissed her wonder. "They're Mr. Wachner's pet owls. He raised them. They must have smelled meat in your groceries."

It was true. A package of chicken parts, wrapped in plastic and bleeding onto their foam diaper, had lain at the top of Jean's grocery bag.

"I save anything dead I find in the woods for them," Mia confided. "Or if a bird flies against our window and kills itself, I take it to the owls." Jean marveled at Mia's self-possession.

For years Jean had observed the Spanish custom of not sitting down to an evening meal before nine o'clock. She had fallen with difficulty into the northern Michigan pattern of noon lunches and six o'clock dinners. But the long, daylight evenings that followed the dinner hour were pleasantly reminiscent of her childhood in Virginia, when she had gathered with the other neighborhood children under the darkening foliage of the broad front yards, thrilled at the privilege of being able to experience the coming-on of night, but relieved not to be alone when it happened.

One evening after dinner Mia offered to take Jean to pick blackberries. Unlike Tim, Mia seemed to have no needs she could not meet herself, and she had been openly hostile to Jean, going out of her way to expose Jean's mistakes. Pleased, Jean hoped the invitation was a sign that Mia no longer regarded her as an intruder.

Jean followed Mia outside, leaving Steve to watch over Tim. Though there was still light, the light seemed to stop at the edge of the woods. Jean was reluctant to move into the shadows, but Mia's first friendly overture seemed too important to refuse. And the easy way Mia moved among the trees shamed her into quickly following her granddaughter.

"Shouldn't we stay on the path?" Jean asked.

"We don't need to. The best berries are off the path. Anyhow, I can tell where we are," Mia said importantly. "We walk toward the big spruce." Jean saw that Mia enjoyed being in charge and decided not to ask further questions. A pelting rain the day before had released the leaves, putting a thick yellow mat on the ground and sending up that dank, earthy smell that was autumn. The fall fragrance filled her with nostalgia. Remembering the autumns of her childhood Jean paid little attention to where Mia was leading her. When at last she looked around and found herself in unfamiliar and darkening woods she hurried to keep up with Mia.

"Now we go this way," Mia ordered. "Tim thought those were Indian graves," she said, pointing to some oval-shaped mounds scattered through the woods. "But Mother said they're just big tree trunks that fell a long time ago and got covered with dirt and then grass grew over them. There *are* Indian burial grounds around here, though. Mr. Wachner showed them to my mother but she won't tell where they are. I know where there's an Indian tree, though."

"What do you mean?" Jean asked. She was glad to be diverted from the uncomfortable feeling the woods gave her and amused at Mia's guided tour. She recalled how Steve too had been like that as a child, eager to tell you what he knew, to *instruct* you. Jean had not been surprised when Steve decided to become a professor.

Mia explained, "The Indians would bend the branch of a tree to show the direction they were taking so other Indians could find their way." Mia jumped from one topic to another: the suction cups on the feet of tree toads, then how the little pile of husks from pine seeds on the stumps of trees were left by squirrels who sat on the stumps and stripped the seeds from the cones. Jean began to feel that Mia was trying to distract her with a rush of information. She could not be sure but twice Mia had appeared to be doubling back on the path as if, knowing Jean's fear of the strange and dark woods, Mia wished to confuse her. Jean tried to put the suspicion out of her mind telling herself Mia was only a child.

The sun was low behind the tops of the trees before Jean heard Mia call out, "Over here, Gran."

The berries Mia pointed out were disappointing. A frost had killed many of the bushes and those that survived had nothing but small, hard fruit. Jean put one tentatively into her mouth. It was seedy, not worth the bother, she thought, but she didn't want to hurt Mia's feelings. The berries were like all the local fruits and vegetables Jean had found since coming north. When she went shopping she was appalled at the meager, blighted produce: hard, rubbery oranges; soft-brown mushrooms; rocklike melons; tomatoes that refused to ripen; and, incredibly, paraffined vegetables much like the wax imitation fruit people used to keep in bowls.

She thought of the market near Dr. Jansen's clinic. Each stall was a still life into which you might enter and move about. Absently she fingered one of the thorny berry branches and wished for a slice of fresh papaya.

Mia's voice jarred her into the present. "You pick here, Gran," Mia directed her. "I'm going to look for a better patch. I'll be right back."

Long minutes passed. Jean stayed where she was for nearly a half hour picking the stingy berries before she was forced to concede that she had been left to find the way home by herself. Jean refused to think the word "malicious." "Malicious" implied there was no reasonable explanation. Mia's behavior had an explanation: she was a ten-year-old child who resented someone's taking her mother's place. Or perhaps *her* place. Jean decided then that when she was sure Tim was completely well she would leave. At the moment, though, the important thing was to find her way back to the cabin.

She tried to guess from which direction they had set out, but she had no idea. Everything in the woods looked alike. She searched for the spruce, but there were several, all equally tall. The bramble scratches on her hands were bleeding. And the dark was coming on quickly.

She told herself it was a forest of small and timid animals and there was nothing to fear. The sensible thing would be to sit down and wait; as soon as he realized she was missing, Steve would come after her. But how embarrassing it would be to have Steve discover her lost in the woods while her ten-year-old granddaughter had made her way home! Resolutely Jean set out in the direction from which she believed they had come.

Lately these woods had found their way into her dreams. In one dream she stood at the edge of the woods, at once terrified of entering them and yet drawn to them, certain she would find Dan there. When the dream recurred she tried to guess its meaning, but entering the dream was as frightening as entering the woods. Her thoughts about Dan's death invariably led her to the moment when Jim Benkin had placed Dan's watch and wallet in her hands. The moment when she knew that somewhere out there was a man who had willed Dan's death.

The light was rapidly leaving the woods. Jean began to hurry toward what she hoped was the direction of Steve's cabin. The trees were a dark tracery against a sky, a mournful shade of mauve.

Too late in the day for birds, the woods were absolutely quiet. It was so hushed that when she saw a light in the distance, it seemed to break into the silence like a sharp sound. She hurried toward it, thinking she had found her way back, but she had not. Unlike Steve's cabin, with its loosened shingles and sagging porch, the cabin she came to looked as if it had been newly made that day. She smelled wood smoke and, thinking of the warmth of a fire, realized she was cold. Impulsively she knocked on the door.

12

Harry Wachner was startled to find Jean Pierce on his doorstep. She was dressed in a casual skirt and sweater, but the style and quality of her clothes belonged to a distant and more exotic world. Her pale hair was twisted into an intricate shape. And there she was, emerging from the woods, with some sort of dangling earrings—of real gold, he was sure. He once felt a similar reaction when he found a parakeet in his maple tree. It didn't belong in the north woods, yet there it was. For several days he had left seeds out for it, hoping to keep the strange bird nearby, but it flew off and had never returned.

"Come in, Mrs. Pierce," he said. "You look a little chilled. Better stand in front of the fire and warm up." It was pleasant to have this attractive woman in his cabin. Since his wife, Phyllis, had died five years ago he had led a bachelor's life, never giving a thought to someone taking Phyllis's place for that did not seem possible. He still carried on conversations with her in his mind. After their years together and their closeness, even in her absence her responses were as predictable as his own.

"I was relieved to see your light," the woman was saying. "Mia and I were out picking blackberries and we got separated. I'm afraid I'm not very good at finding my way around in the woods at night. I hope Mia got home safely."

"That blackberry patch is just a few yards into the woods from your son's cabin. Mia must have taken you the long way around. She oughtn't to have left you. Or maybe you're used to jungles down there where you come from." He was still thinking of the parakeet.

"We lived in the capital. I seldom saw the jungle. Anyhow," she said, with an apologetic smile, "I'm afraid I'm not much of an outdoor person. I was a little frightened out there tonight."

The fire was warming her, flushing some color into her cheeks and lighting her hair, which was either white or blond or a mixture of the two; Harry could not decide. Her eyes were the gray-green of the river where trees hung over the bank.

He wondered how his room looked to her. Plain, he supposed. She would be used to something better. Still, she put up with her son's ramshackle cabin. Certainly his own place was an improvement over that.

He saw Jean examining the room, taking in the books that rested on the pine shelves he had crafted himself. "My wife died five years ago," he told her. "I'm afraid things have gotten a little away from me." His fishing rods and hunting rifles hung from pegs on the walls. His tackle box stood open on a table. Inside the box on a series of trays that opened out, artificial flies were arranged in rows according to their size. "It's attractive—shipshape," Jean said, then laughing at the word. "What I mean is that at Steve's things seem to be falling apart, everything needs attention. I'm not criticizing him. Since his father's death he's been having a bad time."

Harry had heard from Sarah that Steve's dad had been murdered. "Well, I'm not sure things are all that tidy here. I don't suppose you noticed but I raise white mice in my living room." He grinned at her surprise and pointed to a wire cage.

Inside the cage quick white shapes scurried in and out of piles of sawdust. In one corner was a nest of newborn mice that looked like embryonic piglets. Jean was clearly puzzled. "I suppose they're interesting to raise?" She sounded doubtful.

He laughed, "I raise them for my barred owls, so I try not to pay much attention to them. I don't want to get attached—especially now, when I've started to feed them to the owls while the mice are still alive."

Jean shuddered. "Is that necessary?"

"The owls have to learn to hunt and kill or they'll never survive on their own."

"I guess I'd have a hard time choosing between the owls and the mice. How long have you had the owls?"

"Since they were a couple of weeks old. Someone cutting down a hollow tree found the nest and brought them to me."

Jean smiled. "They visited me the other day. I had to hurry in to keep them from taking off with our supper."

"I shouldn't have allowed them to become so tame. I'm afraid it's going to be their undoing—getting close to people. In this world we all need a little suspicion to survive." He had only been making conversation, but the woman was staring at him as though he were voicing her own thoughts. Hurriedly he changed the subject. "Can I get you a cup of hot cider? I make it myself and I'm rather proud of it."

"That would be a treat. I'm still a little cold. Would it be all right for me to call Steve and tell him where I am? I don't want him taking off into the woods after me."

"Go right ahead. Tell him I'll drive you home."

He tried not to eavesdrop on her words of explanation to Steve, but the tone of her voice was apologetic and strained, as though she were talking with a stranger rather than her own son. When she hung up she turned to him. "Steve was relieved to hear I was all right. I'm afraid he was also a little cross with me for being stupid enough to get lost. He was just going out to look for me. Mia told him she ordered me to stay where she left me and I had wandered off."

"And is that what happened?"

Handing her the mug of cider, Harry watched the improbable earrings jiggle as Jean shook her head. "Of course I didn't tell Steve but Mia lost me tonight on purpose. She thinks I'm an intruder. Steve thinks so, too. But that's a secret between you and me." She smiled up at him. "This cider is delicious." She settled into a chair.

"It's pressed from four different kinds of apples to give it just the right taste. I hope you're not going to give up and go away. It's none of my business but it looks to me like Steve could use a little mothering."

"I was planning to leave when Tim recovered but now I've decided to stay until Sarah gets back." She tucked her legs under her and took another sip.

"You look like you're thinking of a secret," he said watching a slow smile spread over her face.

"I was just remembering how we agonized over our wine list when we entertained at the embassy. I wonder what our guests would say to cider. It tastes better to me than the best vintage."

He wondered if she were making fun of him and then decided she was only giving him an honest answer to his question. "I'm sure this is a rather different world than the one you are used to."

"I have to admit that all this empty country is going to take some getting used to. Dan and I always lived in cities," she said, "in

Madrid, and Buenos Aires, and in the capital of Costa Dora."

"Madrid," Harry found pleasure in saying the name of the city. "I always thought I'd like to travel. When I was a kid I dreamed of being a foreign correspondent. Instead I started out as a police reporter in Detroit. All I did was spend my time sitting around in the station waiting for the next murder. I left because after a while you got so bored, you found yourself hoping ..." He stopped himself. What an insensitive and stupid thing to say to a woman whose husband had been murdered! He hurried on. "And I didn't like living in the city. I grew up ten miles from here and I missed the woods and the river. I'd drive up from Detroit every weekend. One Sunday I just decided not to go back.

"I started a newspaper. Around here everyone took the woods and the river for granted. They did what they pleased. Fishing cabins were going up every fifty feet on the river. The runoff from the cabins was destroying the stream. I thought in another few years we could kiss the river good-bye. I believe my paper's made some difference. When you point out the right thing to people, they're prepared to do it."

"I guess I've been out of the States so long," Jean said, "I'd forgotten it was possible to accomplish something by appealing to people's better nature. In the countries I've lived in, an approach like that would be considered naive."

"There's a new problem now. The Valhallists just bought a big chunk of land on the river."

"Valhallists! What are they? I know of the Valhalla in the old Teutonic myths. It was the hall of the gods where the souls of heroes slain in battle or those who died courageously were welcomed. Right? But what does Valhalla have to do with the remote woods of northern Michigan?"

He wondered if she were thinking of her husband and his violent death. He supposed the death of an ambassador murdered in a foreign country might be a kind of battlefield death. "It's a small group, sort of a combination of a survivalists and militia group. I don't have a lot of trouble with that but this group has some nasty racial ideas which they aren't keeping to themselves. There must be about twenty of them living here. They're convinced the world is being destroyed by Blacks and Jews and Muslims. They think we're in for some kind of *Götterdämmerung*. They're getting ready for it—digging bomb shelters, stockpiling food. The worst part is, they're trying to get their Nazi propaganda in the local library. They even wanted to take out an ad in my paper. When the library and I would have nothing to do with them they started distributing leaflets with their racial poison. I've written a couple of articles in my paper about them so they're not too happy with me. With good reason. I'd like them out of here."

Jean winced. "I'm afraid I've grown wary of men with causes. However hateful the Valhallists are, in one thing they might be right: The world does seem chaotic. I've had to struggle not to give up on it. Oddly enough, just when I most needed help with that struggle I met a doctor in Costa Dora who believed enough in people to devote her life to helping them. Somehow her faith was catching. She made me believe that you can answer God back, that you can have a conversation. Since then I haven't stopped talking to him. I hope you'll forgive me for mentioning something so personal but I feel we're friends, someone I've known much longer than a week."

Harry smiled. "I know exactly what you mean. Someone has said you can mention God once at a dinner party, but if you mention God twice you won't be asked back. No matter how much a person thinks about his faith, in polite society the subject is taboo."

All of his life Harry had kept up a running conversation with God. With wry amusement he sometimes felt they were business partners who had ongoing battles of will over how the affairs of their company were going to be run. But no matter how much a part of your life God is, Jean was right. It was awkward to talk about it. Even in that small Lutheran church in which he had been baptized, confirmed, and which he still attended, once the service was over they stood around outside and chatted about the weather or Saturday's football scores.

He smiled at Jean. "I'm glad you feel you can talk with me. I'm enjoying your visit. Perhaps I can talk Mia into losing you again."

Jean laughed. "I won't need Mia's help. I seem to get lost every time I step outside of Steve's cabin. Now I think I had better get back."

"My pickup is just outside."

"I don't like to bother you," Jean protested. "If you point me in the right direction, I'm sure I can find my way back."

Harry would not hear of it. For some time his life had been predictable. He could tell at the beginning of any day what it would bring. And he supposed at his age he ought to be thankful for that. The unexpected was apt to be unpleasant. But here was something new and different. He noticed that Jean, too, seemed to welcome someone to talk to. In her need he had recognized a need of his own. Owls and mice were not much in the way of companionship. He was reluctant to say goodbye to Jean.

As they left the cabin there was a rush of wings and three owls descended to perch on Harry—one on his head, one on a shoulder, and one on his arm, which he automatically extended. After her initial surprise, Jean laughed with pleasure. In the light coming from the cabin windows the three round faces of the owls were framed by whorls of light and dark feathers. The owls bobbed and ducked, holding their heads first on one side and then the other, staring at her with black unblinking eyes. "I suppose they're hungry," she said doubtfully. She clearly did not want to witness the mice being served up.

Seeing her apprehension Harry quickly said, "The owls can wait for their dinner until I get back." He shook the owls loose from his shoulder and arm. In seconds they had disappeared into the woods. He wanted to tell her that when the owls appeared fluttering around him he felt as if one of God's doves was descending. Putting a hand under Jean's arm, he ushered her out to his pickup.

Jean sprang up lightly into the high seat of the truck. "I'm used to getting up on horses," she said in answer to his amused look.

"You and your husband rode?"

"Yes. There were always horses in the countries where we were posted. People with Spanish blood seem to love to ride. Not for the hunting, like the English, but for the elegance. The Spanish are an elegant people."

Harry thought some of that Spanish elegance had rubbed off on her. He drove slowly, but even so the trip took only a few minutes. Before he shut off the motor Harry was surprised to find himself asking, "I don't suppose you'd like to go down the stream this weekend? I have some time on my hands. There aren't many fishermen to guide this time of year. I could show you some of the lovelier parts of this country. It's not all dark woods and blackberry brambles." Then he was afraid that in his attempt to disguise his eagerness he had made his invitation sound too casual.

"The river?" she said. "I'd like that."

It would never have occurred to Harry to look for a woman's companionship, but to refuse it when it presented itself would've seemed ungrateful. He was curious, too, to see how she measured up against the river. That was how he judged everything.

13

Weekdays the family was busy, the children with school and Steve with his job, but Saturdays and Sundays seemed endless to Jean as she coped with Mia's defiance and Steve's moods. On this Saturday Tim was under the kitchen table with a puzzle. Mia was painstakingly sewing doll clothes, struggling with twisted, knotted thread and curtly refusing Jean's offer of help. Steve had been shut in his room with a new book by a South American writer Jean had brought for him hoping to rekindle his interest in literature. Although he often disappeared for an hour or more with the book, Jean couldn't help noticing that the bookmark never advanced. Jean guessed it was not the book that made him disappear into his room, but a need to escape her; he seemed not to want to be in the same room with her. If she was there to keep the family together she was succeeding only in keeping them under the same roof.

Intimidated by the empty woods, too distracted to read, and unwanted or unneeded by those she was asked to watch over, Jean rummaged through the refrigerator and the kitchen shelves. She was determined to create something for dinner to prove that after disasters of rubbery scrambled eggs and gluey pasta she could at last produce something edible. Sarah's cookbook provided a recipe for an apple tart. She saw herself setting a flaky golden circle on the table, its fragrance of cinnamon and apples enchanting Steve and the children. Tucking a towel around her waist, she set to work.

As she began to mix the pastry Tim and Mia edged out the door. Guiltily she realized her last culinary failure had made her cross and unnecessarily short with the children. They hadn't forgotten. She followed the recipe but the dough appeared to have too much flour. When she added water the dough stuck to the board and the rolling pin. The useless mess seemed a metaphor for her efforts with Steve and the children.

If Dan were there he would have put his arms around her and gotten her to laugh, putting the disaster into perspective. Tears streamed down her cheeks and she wiped them off with floury fingers. Hastily, before anyone could discover her failure, she scraped together the remnants of the pastry and threw them in the waste basket. When she turned around she saw Steve watching her, an amused look on his face.

"Why are you making yourself miserable by trying to turn yourself into some sort of a rustic Julia Child? The children could eat hamburgers every day of the week, and if gourmet food was high on my list I wouldn't be living here in the middle of the woods."

Already exasperated and frustrated, Jean blurted out, "What *are* you doing here in the middle of the woods? Why are you letting your brain atrophy, your wife leave you, and your children run wild?" She was afraid he would storm out of the house but he only shook his head.

"You may be angry with me, Mother, but if I answered that question you would hate me and that would be worse."

Jean was too frightened to speak. She only watched as Steve turned and went slowly back to his room, shutting the door between them.

The next afternoon when Harry called Jean with an invitation to spend the afternoon canoeing down the river, Jean eagerly accepted, sure she wouldn't be missed at the cabin. Once on the river she found to her amazement she was actually enjoying herself. The restlessness of the river suited her mood. Riding in the moving canoe, Jean imagined she was on a movie set as she watched the scenery swiftly change around her. Along the bank the maples were slashed with scarlet, the birch and tamarack with gold. There was a wind with an edge to it, but the October sun was warm on their backs. Harry sat behind her, guiding the canoe with a touch of his paddle as the steady current carried them along. A rich river smell rose around them. In the distance bluejays screeched.

"They always sound like rusty hinges to me," Harry said.

A slate-gray bird with an unruly crest swooped down from a dead branch and struck the water with its bill. The bird rose again, a small fish in its mouth, and flew off with a rackety sound. "What's that bird?" Jean asked, startled. There were still many things in the woods that she had not learned to trust.

"A kingfisher. I'm surprised it's still around. They take off for the south about now. Watch it and see if it doesn't keep us company."

It stayed just ahead of them, perching on a dead branch where there were no leaves to obscure its view, darting at the water and moving on to wait for them.

"Why does it stay with us?"

"The canoe scatters the small fish, making them easier for the kingfisher to catch."

Jean found it a great relief to have someone who could answer her questions. Having escaped the tension at the cabin, she had the giddy feeling of someone recovering from a long illness.

For the first mile or two there were fishing shacks on either side of the bank. Then the shacks disappeared and there was no further sign of man. The river that carried them was no more than ten feet at its narrowest, thirty feet at its widest. Jean thought it was nothing like the trickle of muddy water that passed for a river in the country she had left. The water here was like crystal.

They passed grassy islands and swept around hairpin bends. Harry told her the river had once been used to float logs, and from time to time a snagged log appeared in their path. The first time she had cried out, but she saw that Harry knew the exact position of each of the snags and manipulated the canoe around them with a quick stroke of the paddle.

Along the water's edge were shadowy, dark green cedar trees. Then suddenly there was a break in the treeline. On the flat, nearly treeless bank Jean spotted a man standing at attention. He was wearing camouflage fatigues and a military beret. Propped on his shoulder was a rifle. The sight was so unexpected Jean was alarmed into silence. A cold terror crept over her. For a moment she was transported to Costa Dora and the armed soldiers who were everywhere there. She stared dumbly at the man, who was staring back, watching them intently.

Harry explained in a half whisper, "Valhallist. He won't bother us."

The armed man in the soldier's uniform was so much out of place in what Jean had begun to regard as benign wilderness, that the still figure might have been an inanimate display for tourists—a Disney-like re-creation of a bygone time. But, no, the figure was real. The Valhallist's eyes followed them until they were out of sight.

"Idiots!" Harry said. "I should have warned you, but I've grown so used to them, I forgot. That was their camp. They're just playing one of their sick games with those camouflage clothes and guns."

Jean clenched her fists to keep from shaking. "I've been in too many countries where men dressed like that aren't playing at games. Why do they have the guard? What are they afraid of?"

"They think the government is out to get them. I guess they've given up on society."

"Like Steve," she said with a sigh. "Harry, I don't know why he's given up on the world to run away to this wilderness. I'm sure he has some terrible secret that's consuming him, and this isolation isn't helping. It's like those Valhallists—the longer they're away from society, the worse society becomes in their minds, or how could they justify to themselves the sacrifice they're making?"

Harry said, "Maybe you ought to just give Steve a chance to work things out. I don't know that we gain anything by all this explaining of people. It's like the skeletons of the dragonfly nymphs I find on my cabin, something dry and empty left behind to examine while the newly hatched dragonfly has flown off."

As if he needed to take some action Harry put together his fly rod. His line snapped out, touching the water, flicked up again, and was sent out once more. The fly settled lightly a half inch from a grassy log that extended out from the bank. Jean held her breath, uncertain of what to hope for. The fly disappeared below the surface. A moment later a trout broke water, hanging for a fraction of a second suspended in the air. Harry seemed in no hurry to bring the trout in, giving it line, coaxing it toward him, letting it out and finally, at just the moment the trout itself appeared ready, pulling it into the boat. In an hour's time they had five trout.

Harry chose a wooded bluff at a narrow point in the river for their lunch. The pines on either side of the bank were green walls. Looking upstream or down, the walls appeared to converge like green gates closing the river off at both ends, leaving Jean and Harry in splendid isolation.

"It's a lovely place," she said. "Like the last place on earth—or the first."

Harry was feeding bits and pieces of a dead branch into a pile of smoldering leaves and bark. The flame flickered and grew. "For some reason," he said, "the things I usually worry about never bother me on the river. The river takes over."

"Yes," Jean said. "I don't want to sound dramatic, but today is the first day since Dan was killed that everything hasn't been a matter of making choices—whether to get up in the morning or never to get up again, whether to eat or to stop eating altogether." She laughed to cover the desperation in her words. "Right now I'm starved." She watched Harry feeding the fire, thinking that being able to create warmth was surely a great gift. He laid the freshly killed trout on a wire grill. Their flesh was a pale coral but the shimmering bands of pinks and reds and purples had already begun to fade. He covered the trout with slices of bacon and held the grill over the fire. Wherever the fat dripped, a little explosion of flame shot up. The smell of the fire and the bacon was delicious.

He turned to her and in a hesitant voice asked, "I know it's none of my business, but I can't help asking, why would someone want to kill your husband?"

"It was reported as a robbery." Jean was sure she could trust Harry. "It wasn't. There's an active guerrilla movement trying to overturn the Costa Doran government. They want a Marxist state. They resent the United States having anything to do with their country. Somehow the newspapers supporting the guerrillas got hold of a sensational story exposing U.S. involvement in a Costa Doran school that trained the country's security forces. Of course we are only trying to keep peace but the guerrillas didn't see it that way. The security forces have blood on their hands. In the past they've been responsible for thousands of deaths. As the American ambassador, Dan became a target." Jean paused and then looked up at him. "I've never talked with anyone about this, not even Steve."

"How did your husband feel about being involved in something like that?"

There was a note of disapproval in Harry's voice. Jean guessed Harry was a man who would not be comfortable with secrets. "Dan was a realist. He didn't think diplomacy could make a perfect world, but he believed his job could make a difference, and he did it well. He wasn't a conspiratorial man but he liked puzzling things out: second-guessing juntas and revolutions. He thought he was on the right side."

"What did you think of his job?"

"I tried to help him, to keep up the social end of the embassy so it would be one thing he didn't have to worry about. Although I wouldn't be truthful if I told you I didn't worry about Dan. After all, many of the countries we were stationed in were in the midst of some sort of upheaval—war or revolution."

"You won't find things like that happening here," Harry reassured her.

Jean thought of the armed guard at the Valhallists' camp. Even here in this lovely land there were people whose whole life was destruction. But she said nothing.

Harry was concentrating on grilling the trout, which were gold-

en brown now, their tails dark, crisp fans. Jean saw he prided himself on doing things well, as Dan had. The difference was that
there was no danger attached to what Harry did. Jean unwrapped
thick slices of buttered bread. "I saw some watercress on the
stream. Shall I go down and get it to have with the bread?" She
wanted him to know she was finished talking about the past.

He grinned. "The perfect touch."

Jean made her way down the face of the bluff. The current and
wind had eroded the surface so that only sand was left. With each
step the sand fell out from under her feet and she slipped down
the bank at a faster and faster speed. It was great fun. She felt
young and a little reckless. A thick green mat of watercress grew
along the edge of a log. She placed a foot on the log to steady herself as she bent over the water. The log, which had appeared firmly
anchored, rolled, plunging her into the icy river. The water came
only to her waist. Somehow the whole accident seemed hilarious,
the kind of thing you knew immediately would be laughed about
for years to come, except that she was terribly cold. But there was
something else. The sudden shock of the water took her breath
away, startling her out of her feelings of depression and hopeless-
ness. She felt reborn in the river, as if all her doubts had been
washed away. She felt something she had not felt for months—
hopeful.

Jean saw Harry half run, half slide down the bank. Deliberately
she grabbed a handful of watercress, and laughing, started up the
bank to meet him. He held her firmly by the arm and guided her
toward the fire.

Her teeth began to chatter. "You must think I'm a terrible
klutz," she said.

But he was not smiling. "Suppose the water had been deep

there, in this strong current you could have drowned."

She was touched by his concern. It seemed a long time since anyone had worried about her. He unbuttoned his wool shirt and gave it to her. "It's extra long. You get your wet things off, I'm going down to the canoe and get a blanket."

She unpeeled the soggy, clinging clothes and slipped into the warm wool shirt. When he returned Harry draped the blanket around her. She unpinned her long hair and wrung out the water; then she knelt by the fire, and bending her head to let her hair fall over her face, began spreading it with her fingers to dry it, aware that Harry was watching her. The fire was hot on her face and hands. In a few minutes she pushed her hair back from her face and said, "I'm starving."

"I forgot to bring the paper plates from the canoe. Should I go after them?" he asked.

"No. We'll do without. If you fall in, I can't very well give you the shirt off *my* back."

They smiled at each other. She accepted one of the trout, and holding the hot fish gingerly in her fingers, tore a piece of the flesh from its backbone. It was moist and sweet and the skin crisp, tasting of bacon and wood smoke. She finished it quickly.

"These fish are the best I've ever had," she said.

"It's the best watercress I've ever had," he teased.

The cress was much more peppery than the bunches she was used to in the capital. For dessert they had cookies. She had made them herself, although it had taken a concerted effort and several disasters. "When you've tasted these, you've sampled my entire repertoire," Jean joked. The cookies crumbled in their hands as they ate them. Harry smiled at her. He bent over and kissed her lightly on her cheek, still warm from the fire. Then, embarrassed, he began to gather the leftovers from the picnic lunch and carry them down to the canoe, leaving her to get into her dried clothes.

For the first time since her husband's death, Jean felt Dan's presence. *We are all connected,* she thought. From the beginning of time love has been the link, the continuum. She had not expected to feel love again. She had seen love as a great danger for anything that touched the person you loved would touch you; if something destroyed that person it would destroy you. Now, cautiously, tentatively, she wondered if the risk might be worth it and then, haunted by old fears, decided it would not be.

14

It is nearly impossible for people who have learned manners to live in a small house day in and day out without finding a way to get along. Although there was not a moment when he did not miss Sarah, Steve was beginning to find breakfasts almost pleasant. On this November morning as an early autumn storm tore the last leaves from the trees the four of them sat around the breakfast table, the fire he had built in the stove warming the room.

Tim anguished over what kind of cereal he wanted that morning, making a face at Mia's toasted cheese sandwich. "That's disgusting."

"In Europe," Jean told Tim, "they often eat cheese for breakfast."

Mia gave Jean a rare smile. "See, you don't know it all," she told Tim with a superior voice.

Steve was relieved to see that Jean and Mia had achieved a truce. Jean purposely deferred to Mia, going for walks with her and listening to her with genuine interest as she lectured Jean on trees. Mia was reading her way through a 1912 edition of a woodsman's guide that had come with the cabin.

Steve knew that the children were not as free as they thought. With subtle questions indifferently put, Jean managed to know where they were and what they were doing. She appeared to leave decisions to them, but Steve sensed, as did the children, a nearly invisible boundary around the edges of their freedom. It formed a fastness they were all beginning to count upon.

As Steve watched his mother with the children he was surprised at how well she was beginning to master tasks that in his own child-hood had been the responsibility of servants. He found himself faintly jealous of her attentions to the children, attentions of which he had often been deprived.

If he was ambivalent about Jean's attentions toward the chil-dren, he was even more unsure of how he felt about his mother and Harry Wachner. Nearly every Saturday she announced it was her "day off" and accompanied Harry on his partridge shoots or his prowls around the countryside. When she came home in the evening her face was flushed, her eyes bright, like an infatuated schoolgirl, Steve thought somewhat bitterly.

He could not see what his mother had in common with Harry. After all, she was a woman of impeccable tastes. He remembered afternoons when he was Mia's age, coming home from the American school in Buenos Aires to find women in for tea. His mother, speaking perfect Spanish, would be dressed in something simple and understated, a pale wool suit or a silk dress in a muted color, the gold bangles on her arm ringing softly as she passed around cups of tea. It was impossible to reconcile those childhood memories with the woman who had taken to wearing Sarah's old jeans and flannel shirts and who had proudly shown off her new expertise in plucking the partridges and ducks with which Harry gifted them.

It was even more difficult to understand his mother's attraction toward a man who was so unlike his father. Steve could not imagine Harry anywhere but here. His father had been a man of the world, fluent in several languages, graceful and deadly on the tennis and squash courts, where he had always been able to defeat Steve. A private man, Dan did not seem to enjoy either the sport or the competition. But he had also understood that in his business you had to have friends—or more accurately, contacts. It was his father's conviviality, the diplomatic and seemingly apolitical part of his job, that had for so many years enabled Steve to deny that his father was involved in matters that could cause countries to rise or fall. After a man of the world like his father, what could his mother possibly see in a rustic like Harry Wachner?

* * *

Jean could not decide how she felt about Harry. Curled up comfortably on Harry's couch one afternoon, she marveled at the delicate movements of Harry's square, rather stubby fingers as they looped what appeared to be an invisible thread around a bit of feather. He added a few mink hairs. "It's like creation," she said. "Do you think God took that much trouble over each fly *he* made?"

"Only if he was a trout fisherman," Harry said and laughed. "Trout are particular." He asked, "Would you like me to teach you how to fish this spring?"

Jean hesitated. Once you love someone, you have to live with the fear of losing him. She wasn't ready to face that again. She tried to keep her voice impersonal. "I'm afraid I won't be here this spring. I'll be leaving when Sarah gets back. Sarah and Steve need time to work things out. I'll be sorry to go and that surprises me. When I first came, this place seemed like the end of the world. You've changed that—you and Mia and Tim."

"Could you spend the rest of your life in a place like this?"

Harry was bent over the vise that held his trout fly, but Jean could see his face was flushed.

"I'm not sure. I've been thinking about moving to a city—Boston or Chicago. There are things I've missed in Costa Dora—music, a decent library, museums. My father was the director of a small but quite good museum in Virginia. I spent my childhood in his museum. He'd take me with him on days when the place was closed. It was a strange kind of setting for a child's play, a place always quiet and in perfect taste. Everything was unique and rare and couldn't be touched." She smiled at Harry. "I suppose that's why the country around here takes so much getting used to for me—thousands of trees, millions of plants and insects." It was as though she were thinking aloud. "After Dan's death I found myself thinking what happens is all random. A museum with no curator, no God making careful choices."

Harry put his hand over hers. "All those millions of trees and plants and insects are survival insurance. And none of it is random, not if you look closely. Actually the variety is awesome—not the way kids use the word 'awesome' but in its real meaning—it fills you with wonder. You don't walk into a museum full of great works of art and think they are random acts. I can take you for a walk in the woods with a magnifying glass and show you things that surpass in color and design anything you could find in the best museum in the world. Random?" He shook his head. "No."

"I'm just beginning to find my faith again. I think it was your river. But I feel so vulnerable I need to build a shell around me like those caddis nymphs you told me about." Harry had shown her how on the river bottom the caddis nymphs surrounded themselves with an armor of bits of stone.

Harry's voice was encouraging. "I suppose the caddis nymph

could stay safely on the bottom of the river. Instead it sheds its shield and explodes out of the water even though it only has twenty-four hours to live. It chooses life at whatever cost, I think. You'd make the same choice."

The phone rang. Harry answered it, but after a moment he slammed the receiver down, his face tightened to hold back anger. "That's the third threatening call I've had today. Those dim-witted Valhallists. It's like them to do something underhanded like that."

"Is it the article you wrote?" Jean had seen the front-page story in Harry's newspaper condemning the propaganda in the leaflets the Valhallists were passing out. The leaflets were full of racial hatred. "Isn't it dangerous tangling with people who walk around with guns?" Jean had a sudden feeling of *déjà vu*. Hadn't she said similar words more than once to Dan? One of the pleasures in her relationship with Harry had been her belief that she need not be afraid for him. She reached for her jacket. She didn't want to worry over Harry as she had once worried over Dan. "I hate to leave, but I have to go back. Steve tends to wait up for me—I can't think why."

But she did know. Steve disapproved of her relationship with Harry. He guessed she cared for Harry. These last weeks Jean had warned herself that Harry was becoming too important to her. She tried to imagine if it would be possible to live in a place like this. Was she really finished with the large places of the world? And "large" in what sense? Only in the sense that you lost yourself more easily in a city, whereas here you could not lose yourself at all. There were almost no distractions. The farther you walked through the empty countryside the closer you came to yourself. This isolated world had been an inward journey and getting to know herself hadn't been easy. She marveled at Harry's steady faith. He was comfortable with himself. If he sometimes shook his fist at the world there was no malice in his anger, only impatience.

As she walked with Harry toward Steve's cabin, Jean, taking advantage of the anonymity of the dark woods, tried to tell Harry how angry she had been with God when Dan had been killed, how she had gone from church to church to accuse him in all his homes. "I must have been very foolish."

Harry took her arm. "I've never found talking with God foolish." Suddenly he stopped, tightened his grip on her arm and ordered, "Stand still." Directly ahead of them a light moved along, sweeping from side to side through the woods—a high-powered flashlight. For a moment Jean thought Steve had come out to meet them. The light came closer until they were caught in its beam. At the same moment, Harry called out "Taking a little walk, Crites?" The light snapped off as quickly as a snuffed match.

There was a silence and then a grudging answer: "Just looking for a raccoon." After her eyes recovered from the beam of Crites' flashlight, Jean could see in the pale moonlight a man standing a short distance away, a rifle under his arm. Harry said, "You don't need a deer rifle to get a raccoon, Crites. And where's your dog? I would have thought you'd have your dog along on a coon hunt."

Harry's voice was even, almost pleasant, but Crites' reply was indignant and angry. "I don't need you to tell me how to hunt raccoon."

Jean watched Crites walk away, anger in every step. His resentment made Jean feel *they* were the intruders. For a while she was silent, sensing Crites had not gone far but was skulking nearby, waiting to hear what was said about him. "What was he doing?" she asked Harry in a low voice.

"He was shining deer. The deer are attracted to the light. When they come out of the woods he shoots them. It's illegal and it's poor sportsmanship. He's doing a little 'deerjacking,' trying to get his deer before the season starts and the hunters get up here from downstate and scare the deer into the cedar swamps. I suppose I should be angrier at him. I have plenty to say about poachers in the newspaper. But he's out of a job and I know he needs the meat. Still, he's a good shot. He wouldn't have too much trouble getting a deer the same way the rest of us do, and people would think a lot more of him."

Harry had not lowered his voice and Jean felt sure that Harry knew Crites was somewhere nearby. Harry meant Crites to hear every word.

After she had said good night to Harry, Jean switched on the light in the dark cabin to discover Steve sitting by himself in the living room. The fire had gone out. He sat sprawled in a chair, half asleep. She wanted to ask him what he had been thinking of there in the dark, but she only said, "We saw Mr. Crites in the woods. He was shining deer."

"I thought I made it clear to him that I don't want to see him anywhere around here. It's too dangerous with Mia and Tim roaming around in the woods. Anyhow, this is private property. I'm the one who pays taxes on it, not Crites."

"I have a feeling he doesn't like being told to stay out." As she spoke Jean couldn't help remembering how Steve had always insisted on the rights of the Costa Doran peasants to land. Now that he had his own land he had changed his mind. She said nothing more, but told him instead about the Valhallists. "I worry about Harry. He's been getting threatening phone calls because of that article."

Steve shrugged off the calls. "It's hard to take those Valhallists seriously. They seem like children playing some sort of game."

That night in her dreams it was the Valhallists that cornered Dan and began shooting. She cried out in her sleep, awakening Tim, who was a light sleeper. He wandered into her room, his arms full of stuffed animals. Long after she comforted him and got him back to bed she sat up wondering how she could hope to protect everyone under her care. Tim had insisted on leaving one of his stuffed animals for her, a threadbare wolf with one missing ear. Jean reached for the worn animal and, strangely comforted, fell asleep.

15

Hazen Crites backed his truck gently out of his driveway, for the shocks on the ramshackle vehicle were nearly shot. The muffler hung down, scraping along the gravel road. Inside the truck Crites looked sadly at the black hole where a radio used to play country music that soothed him as nothing else ever had. The seat beside him was covered with hair from his hunting dogs and the windshield was smeared with their nose prints. Crites put the car in gear and headed toward the Pierces'.

He had meant to get one buck the night before the season opened and one legally, all on Pierce's property. Two bucks would feed them through the winter. He had not planned to ask Pierce's permission to hunt there the morning of opening day, but since last night's confrontation with Harry and Pierce's mother he decided he would go directly to Pierce. Crites had overheard Harry describe him as a good shot who could get a buck openly like anyone else. So that's what he'd do. It might be that Pierce would say no. He would hunt on the land anyhow.

Steve Pierce appeared at the door before Crites had an opportunity to knock. It took him aback. Behind Pierce he could see Pierce's mother and the children sitting around a table. "I suppose you don't care if I hunt on your property tomorrow?" he blurted out.

Pierce's voice was impatient. "I thought I was very clear when I told you I don't want anyone with a gun on my property."

Seeing that the mother was frowning and appeared upset at her son, Crites persisted. "Well, I could wait till your kids are in school, so I don't see there'd be any problems. It would just be for opening day." Crites heard a whining note creep into his voice and attempted a more nonchalant manner. "If you're thinking of the deer, you got to keep them down, otherwise they just starve over the winter. Anyone'll tell you that." *Let the man see he didn't know everything,* Crites thought.

"The answer is no, Crites, and the next time you try to shine deer around here, we'll call the conservation officer."

Crites pulled out of the driveway, wheels churning up sand, in an effort to get away as fast as possible. The truck bucked and he heard a clanking noise. The muffler had fallen off. He roared ahead, refusing to give them the satisfaction of seeing him turn back to retrieve it. He was more determined than ever to get his deer on Steve Pierce's property.

* * *

The morning was still dark as Mia and Tim pulled on their coats and boots. "The school bus won't be here for another ten minutes," Jean cautioned them.

"I know, but it *snowed* last night. It's the first big snow," Mia said, pushing Tim out the door in front of her.

Steve came into the kitchen, his down jacket looking like a life preserver on his thin body. He gave Jean a sheepish grin. "Look," he said, "will you do something for me? Call Hazen Crites and tell him I said it was all right for him to hunt here after the children leave for school. I don't much like the image of myself as *El Grande Señor.*"

Jean smiled with relief. "I didn't think the image fit you myself. I'll be sure the children don't go into the woods after school. Will you be home for dinner?"

"Probably not. With the snow we'll be working overtime to keep the roads clean. We don't want a bunch of boozed-up hunters skidding all over the highway."

"What do you think about all day, alone in the plow?" Jean ventured.

"Most of the time I don't think, which is why it's such a good job. If I catch myself thinking, I turn on the radio." Steve threw a grin over his shoulder and, opening the door to the flying snow, left.

Jean went to the window and watched Steve clear the snow from the truck and back it out onto the road. Mia and Tim waved to him. Tim sent a snowball flying after the truck. Both children were covered with snow, and she wondered if she ought to call them in and have them dry off. She looked at her watch. The bus was due any minute, though it might be running a little late because of the weather. She decided against taking a chance and having the children miss it.

It was nearly daylight and the hunters would be starting into the woods. She thought about Harry. He was hunting today, too. She hoped he would be safe. Remembering Hazen Crites, she hurried to the phone, pleased to be able to pass along Steve's message. When Mrs. Crites said her husband had already left, Jean was disappointed. "If you talk with him, Mrs. Crites, tell him Steve said he was welcome to hunt here, but of course, not until the children are off to school."

Jean poured herself another cup of coffee and took it to the window. Everything outside was white: trees, sky, earth. Although the wind was moving the snow through the air horizontally, it somehow managed to cover the ground. The children were gone. The bus had come on time after all. It was a good thing she had not called them in.

* * *

Tim's mittens were already soggy from throwing snowballs. He heard a motor approach and looked expectantly through the clouds of snow, thinking the bus was coming. But it was only Mr. Crites' beat-up truck. He and Mia watched as Crites turned onto the trail that led into their woods.

"He's not supposed to be on our property," Mia said indignantly. "He's trespassing. I'll bet he wants to hunt on our land. I heard Dad tell him yesterday he wasn't supposed to. I'm going to see where he's headed. Come on, Tim."

"We'll miss the bus," Tim pleaded. He was wriggling to dislodge a piece of snow that had worked its way down the back of his shirt.

"The bus'll be late because of the snow."

"I don't care. I'm not going with you." The wind had increased and the blowing snow stung his face. Tim thought longingly of the warm interior of the bus.

"You don't care *what* happens to our property," Mia accused. "You heard Dad say he doesn't want Mr. Crites hunting here. Someone has to guard our land." She started running toward the trail where the tracks from Crites's truck were rapidly disappearing.

Tim watched Mia disappear into the white woods. He thought of going after her, even of running back to the house to tell on her, but the flashing lights of the school bus appeared through the snow. The bus door opened welcoming him into its warmth.

* * *

Hazen Crites eased his pickup in and out of the snow-covered ruts. He would take the truck just far enough so that it could not be seen from the road or the Pierces' house and no farther. It wouldn't do to have the deer scared off by the chugging and wheezing of the motor. When he had his buck and had dressed it out, he could drive in and throw the carcass into the bed of the truck.

He always worked himself up on opening day. Right now he was so excited he was finding it a little hard to breathe. It was the one day when he was sure of finding a little success. It wasn't just luck, either. He worked for it. He'd been back here every morning for days, spying on that old buck. Crites knew just where he would be. He had found plenty of rubs and scrapes from him.

When Crites had seen the snow that morning he thought it would be perfect tracking weather. Now he was not so sure. It was coming down too fast. There were a good five inches of heavy, wet snow on the ground. It had piled up on the branches of the trees. Under its weight the lower limbs touched the ground. He looked behind him. Sure enough, his footprints were nearly covered up. There was going to be too much snow to track the buck. What was more, in this weather the buck might just stay in hemlock cover, not even moseying out onto the trail.

Crites listened for the least sound, a snapping twig or the buck's snort. When a sound came, it was from the wrong direction, not the direction from which he expected the buck to appear. Still, he wasn't taking chances and by the time he faced in the direction of the sound, his rifle was in place. He saw a movement at the top of the hill over which he had just made his way. He slipped the bolt, pleased at how easily it moved under his hand. No one kept his gun in better condition. Whatever was moving was too small for a deer, even a yearling, and he saw a spot of color.

It was the Pierce brat. She had followed him into the woods! She'd spook the buck for sure and his opening day would be ruined. The worst thing about what was happening to him was his lack of surprise. Something had warned him this last bit of pleasure would be taken from him. Once all the action of opening day had passed the deer took off for cover and it was hard to get to them.

He wasn't really surprised by this stroke of bad luck. He saw the day going to pieces. What if he didn't get his buck? What if someone else tracked it down? For one brief moment in his fury he considered pulling the trigger. He could say it was an accident. Accidents happened every day during the deer season.

Impulsively he raised his gun, then nearly dropped it in his haste to keep himself from doing something unthinkable. He was shaken by how quickly things changed direction.

He was sure she couldn't see him. She was trying to follow his tracks, moving slowly, having trouble because the snow was covering them over so quickly. He could lead her away from where he meant to go. He started running along a narrow trail that spurred off at a right angle from the way he had been headed.

He came to a thick grove of white pine and hemlock. Crites swept away his tracks with a pine branch and shinnied up a hemlock trunk, pulling himself from one branch to the next, the whole operation awkward because of his gun. The branches were thick and close together. Even if she looked up, she probably could not see him.

After a bit her small figure appeared over a rise. It disgusted him to think a little girl had chased him up a tree. He tensed as she got closer. Keeping perfectly still was almost impossible; snow was settling on his face. His eyelashes were so flocked, he could hardly see. She was under his tree and then she was moving away. In a moment or two she would be out of sight and he could circle back. He believed now he would get his buck, but this time he was careful to warn himself against feeling too optimistic.

* * *

When Mia came to the grove of hemlock trees the faint tracks she was following disappeared. She wondered if Mr. Crites had turned off the path into the woods, but there were no footprints to suggest he had. When she looked in the direction from which she thought she had come, there were no tracks at all. She had been so intent on following Mr. Crites, she hadn't noticed where she was going. Now she knew she would have difficulty finding her way back. It seemed better to go forward and catch up with her quarry, and then he would lead them both back. It did not occur to her that he might be too angry to lead her anywhere, that he might resist being taken into her custody. She was sure she had right on her side and that was all that was necessary.

It's odd, Mia thought, *how different the woods appear in winter.* She knew all the trails, but it was the summer trees she knew and not the stark emptiness of the winter ones. Familiar landmarks—fallen logs, patches of fern and ground pine, stands of wild honey-suckle and juniper—had disappeared under the snow. This disappearing act gave Mia an eerie feeling. She didn't want to vanish from the world in the company of Hazen Crites. She saw she was not moving fast enough. She tried to run but the trail was uphill. After a few minutes she gave up running. Her feet were like chunks of ice; she couldn't even feel her toes when she wiggled them. Her cheeks were raw with wind and cold. She realized she had stopped moving and was standing still. The snow was heavier than ever. In the distance she heard the sharp crack of a rifle. Startled, she tried to decide from which direction it had come but the world around her seemed to have lost all direction.

* * *

Summoned to the principal's office and asked where his sister was, Tim was sure he ought not to tell the truth. He had already let Mia down once today by not helping her chase Mr. Crites from their property. Skipping school was a serious offense. "Mia's sick in bed with a sore throat," he said, expecting the secretary to see through his lie at once.

"Well, if she's going to be out tomorrow, Tim, you tell your grandmother to be sure to call us first thing in the morning."

Tim rejoined his class in the gym. They were playing his favorite game with the parachute given to the school by a child's father who had been in the Air Force during the Gulf War. The game was called "Floating Cloud." Everyone took hold of the parachute. At a signal from their teacher, they swung the chute over their heads as high as they could and let go. If they did it well, it sometimes floated right up to the top of the gym roof. Then they all huddled together and let the light silk chute drift down over them as softly as falling snow.

At eleven o'clock, the principal, Mr. Peterson, announced over the loud speaker that because of the snow, school would be dismissed at noon. There was a cheer from the classrooms. Tim heard one teacher say to another, "Peterson has figured out that if he dismisses us by noon he can be in the woods looking for a buck by twelve thirty. He probably planned to let us out this morning when he got up and saw the snow. Bet he's got his hunting gear in the car."

16

The entire crew of the dig had been invited to a wedding. Ernesto, one of the archaeologists from the Costa Doran university, was getting married in the old capital. His bride, Sofía, was the daughter of a wealthy owner of a sugar refinery. In a grand gesture the father of the bride had rented a plane to fly everyone on the dig down to the old capital for the ceremony. After weeks of crowded dormitory living, Sarah was luxuriating in her own room in a fashionable hotel, another amenity furnished by the bride's father.

Sarah reveled in the waves of cool breezes from the air conditioner. Then she took a long hot shower. For once she did not have to worry about conserving water. She emptied the little bottle of complimentary hotel body lotion and rubbed it lavishly over her red, peeling arms and shoulders. Then she wrapped herself in a terry robe and hopelessly surveyed the possibilities in her wardrobe. She hadn't packed any dressy clothes when she left the States and would have to make do with a dark skirt and a white blouse fancied up with a chiffon scarf someone had lent her. She was looking forward to the wedding, which she knew would be elegant.

The ceremony was held in an eighteenth century church. A part of the church, destroyed two centuries before by a devastating

earthquake, still lay in ruins, a symbol for all that country's cata-
strophes. The rebuilt part of the church where the ceremony took
place boasted soaring columns and arches and an ornate altar-
piece covered with gold leaf. The bride, swathed in white satin and
lace, looked like an exquisite doll. Ernesto, who had never been
seen at the digs in anything but jeans and a grubby T-shirt, was
immaculate in a morning coat and striped trousers. The urbane
guests who had come up that morning from the Costa Doran capital in their Mercedes and Jaguars and limousines were dressed in
the latest fashion and draped with gold. Even one of the Costa
Doran presidential candidates was there. Observing it all with a
mixture of awe and amusement, Sarah thought the guests, dressed
for a ceremony in their necklaces and earrings of gold, were not
so different from the ancient Maya who had once lived there.

Following the wedding, Sofía and Ernesto were transported by
horse and carriage to a restaurant that had once been a convent.
Now its great stone walls and gardens were transformed into a luxury hotel. The interior was furnished in heavy chests and massive
refractory tables. It was lit by hundreds of candles so that you felt
you were in a place of worship and that the bell captains and wait-
ers were padding about on holy ground.

Everything about the reception was resplendent, richly embroidered with the trappings of wealth. There were armfuls of Calla
lilies everywhere and trays loaded with glasses of vintage cham-
pagne. The orchestra alternated between Viennese waltzes and
frenetic Latin rhythms.

A reporter accompanied by a photographer went from table to
table, lingering at the table of the presidential candidate. A con-
troversial candidate, he was under the constant surveillance of
four burly guards. When the reporter reached Sarah's table he

turned to his photographer and in rapid Spanish said, "José, take the señorita's picture. Turning to her he asked first in Spanish and then in English, "Please, could I have your name?"

Sarah, proud of her Spanish, replied in that language, "I'm afraid I am *'nadie,'* nobody." She had learned her Spanish as a child so that she had almost no accent.

The reporter, a young man who obviously admired Sarah, continued to ask questions. "You are a friend of the bride? The groom?"

Sarah explained, "I'm here working on a dig with the groom, Ernesto."

The reporter asked in a friendly voice, "Where is this dig?"

"In the northern part of the country near the border."

"What do you find?" he asked, his voice skeptical. "The odd piece of pottery? A lot of effort and money for not very much result?"

Eager to defend the dig, Sarah said, "On the contrary. We made this marvelous find." She described the warrior.

"Do you think I could get a picture of it?" the reporter asked. "I might do a story on it. I suppose if I came north to visit the digs you'd be kind enough to show me around?"

Amused at his attention, but feeling it had gone far enough, Sarah said, "Professor Reisner would take you in hand. He loves telling people about the dig."

The reporter's interest in a visit to the dig seemed to vanish. Instead he wanted to know, "How long will you be down here in the old capital? I might call you and we could have dinner."

Sarah shook her head. "We're going back to the dig first thing in the morning." She smiled at him. "Perhaps sometime when my husband and I are here we can all have dinner together."

The reporter looked disappointed. "That's not what I was hoping for, but please tell your husband how fortunate he is." The reporter and his trailing shadow of a photographer moved on to photograph an attractive woman at the next table.

Late in the evening when Sarah returned to her pleasant room in the elegant hotel she had to face the fact that all day her pleasure in the festivities had been accompanied by a counterpoint of guilt. She could not help thinking of the simplicity of the wedding ceremonies she had witnessed as a child at the mission, the groom in a dark suit, its age giving it a greenish tinge, the bride in a traditional skirt and blouse heavy with embroidery, and a simple wedding feast of beans and tortillas and homemade beer.

The wealthy landowners at Ernesto's wedding were very like the men who had made life so miserable for Maria's family—as well as all of the people in her village. Two percent of the population owned 70 percent of Costa Dora's land. Those same landowners were clothed with *impunidad,* impunity. They controlled the government, the army, the police, and most of the newspapers.

In the small Costa Doran village in which Sarah had lived, families often awoke at three in the morning and, after a meager breakfast, climbed into crowded trucks and were driven to the coffee plantation where they picked coffee in the hot sun, the very youngest children picking from the lowest branches. It was delicate work. The beans had to be tenderly grasped or one of the fragile branches might be damaged and the pay of the worker docked by an overseer. At the end of the grueling day the workers were paid in pennies and charged outrageously for any food or supplies they purchased from the landowner's *cantina.*

In years past it had been landowners, like those she had met at the wedding, who waited until the villagers had labored for months to clear a little land for planting and then came to claim the land for their own, running off the Maya. Anyone who protested was imprisoned by the government. She thought of Steve and knew he would understand what she was feeling. But where she wanted justice, Steve had wanted retribution. What he felt now, she had no idea. Since his father's death, he had refused to discuss Costa Doran politics.

The next morning, the archaeological staff, tired from partying and sorry to leave the luxury of the hotel, headed reluctantly for the airport. On the plane someone handed Sarah the morning edition of the country's leading newspaper. Because everything the presidential candidate did was news, the coverage of the wedding was on page one. It wasn't the photographs of the candidate that caught Sarah's eye. It was her own picture with a caption naming her and explaining she was working at the same dig as the groom where an invaluable statue had been found. A short description of the warrior followed. Sarah smiled to see herself described as the *"bella"* Señora Pierce. Evidently the reporter had forgiven her rebuff. She carefully tore out the picture to send on to Steve.

After the excitement of the wedding Sarah found it hard to get back into the routine of the dig. The sun seemed hotter, the dormitories more austere, the food dull. Her worry about Steve and her separation from the children made the days endless. *I should never have come,* Sarah upbraided herself. She tried to imagine what the children were doing, going over their familiar routine in her mind, desolate at her separation from them. She waited more impatiently than ever for letters from home, hungry for the scribbled notes she guessed the children sent only because Jean stood over them. The hunting season would be on now—there might even be snow.

With the sun beating down and heat encasing her like hot armor, Sarah found winter hard to imagine.

Even more difficult to imagine was her return to Steve. His letters were cold and non-committal. There was no indication that they would be going back to the university. She had all but made up her mind to take the children and leave Steve to his angry moods and wasted life when one afternoon her roommate, Louise, announced, "Letter for you." Sarah hurried to the table where a small pile of letters was stacked each day by whomever made the trip into town for supplies and mail. She hoped for a letter from Steve, or at least one of Jean's conscientious missives filled with assurances that the children were fine and with descriptions of all the daily happenings Sarah could pour over.

The letter was not from home. And oddly it had no stamp, so it must have been hand delivered. Curious, Sarah pushed her disappointment aside. She tore open the sealed envelope and pulled out a sheet of cheap paper. She read the letter twice, unable the first time to believe her eyes:

Señora Pierce,

Please be so kind as to meet with me tomorrow afternoon at the Café Amigos at one in the afternoon. I have some important information about your husband. Do not tell of the meeting to anyone or there will be <u>very</u> <u>dangerous</u> consequences for him. We have met once before when you came to visit us in the hills.

Respectfully,
Carlos

Sarah quickly hid the note in its envelope, wishing she could make it disappear forever. She hurried outside where she could be alone, dropping down on a wooden bench beneath a cedar tree. A small, pale-green lizard was sunning itself on the bench, and Sarah kept to one side so as not to disturb it. She envied the lizard its mindless repose. On some unconscious level she thought that perhaps if she were kind to the lizard, God would be kind to her and make the letter vanish.

Sarah had heard the guerrillas were nearby. Painted on the walls of the buildings in the small village near the digs were the familiar initials of their organization and their slogan: *Solidaridad.* She thought of the night she and Steve had spent with the guerrillas and the way Carlos had looked at Steve. She remembered the hate in his eyes and his pretended friendship. Whatever he had to tell her about Steve would be malicious. Yet, knowing how tortured Steve was, she was eager to find out anything that might help him.

The next day she could think of nothing but her meeting with Carlos. She carelessly stepped on a bit of pottery, crunching it under her shoe, and then began to cry at its destruction. Professor Reisner told her to go back to the dormitory and lie down. "That's not like you, Sarah, you must be coming down with something," he said.

Quickly she agreed, using the imagined illness as an excuse to request the van to go into town for some medicine. They all took turns using the van to run into the village for sunscreen or soap or a stop at the post office for stamps. Professor Reisner offered to send someone with her but she shook her head. "Honestly, I'm fine. Just a little tummy trouble. I know what to get."

The dirt road was dry and dust came in through the floorboards and the cracks in the doors of the van. A fine flour of dust settled on her bare arms and legs and she could feel grit on the steering wheel. The cloud of dust obscured her view and coated the bushes along the road. Even the sunlight was veiled with dust. It was no better in the village. Everything there had a parched look. The grass seemed brittle. The few trees appeared to have been defoliated by some disease and gave no shade.

People moved slowly, almost cautiously in the dry heat. With November, the *verano*, the dry summer season, had arrived. She parked near the town square where a band of half-starved dogs loped along the street. Three schoolgirls sat on one of the benches, their handwoven *huipiles* lovely enough for any museum. From the pattern of embroidery on the blouses she could tell one of the girls was from the village where she and her parents had lived. The village was not more than thirty miles from the dig. Perhaps she would ask for the van one day and drive there to revisit her childhood home. She thought back wistfully to the days when she believed the answers to everything in life could be found in the simple lessons her mother taught in their Sunday school held under the broad shade of the ceiba trees. *How*, she wondered, *did everything get so complicated?*

The townspeople were used to the archaeologists coming into town and paid little attention to Sarah as she walked across the square. Moving from the white light into the darkness of the café she was blinded for a moment and couldn't make out the faces of the people seated at the tables. Not wanting to appear to be searching for someone, she seated herself at a table near the entrance. She had just ordered a Coke when a man came from the back of the café and pulled out the chair across from her.

"Permitame," he said to her and then turned to the waiter and pointed at her Coke. *"Dos,"* he said before seating himself across from her. For a moment she didn't recognize Carlos. His beard had been shaven off, and he wasn't dressed in camouflage but in khaki slacks and a cotton shirt in a jarring green print. His smile was as she recalled—broad but not deep. He spoke with stilted English.

"Señora, it has been some time since I spent a pleasant evening together with you and your husband. Imagine my surprise and delight to see that you were back in our country again. I understand your husband is not with you."

"No. He had to stay at home. We have two children." At once she was sorry to have mentioned the children, sorry to have given this man any information about her life.

"Steve takes care of the children?" There was derision in his voice.

She was too nervous for this small talk. "You have something to tell me about Steve?"

There was silence while the waiter placed two Cokes on the table. Pouring hers she was disappointed to find the can was lukewarm. During the hot drive she had looked forward to an icy cold drink. Nothing seemed to be going right.

"You Americans are always in such a hurry to get to the point." He leaned closer to her and Sarah could smell a cheap perfume, from shaving cream or something he used on his hair. She had to keep herself from drawing back. He noticed her distaste and, giving her a scathing look, said, "Perhaps it is just as well that we don't spend too much time together."

Sarah sat motionless as he told the story. Enduring it gave her the same feeling she had had years ago as a child when she had broken a tooth and the dentist had to cut her gum and extract the root. He was a local man from Costa Dora and had not used enough anesthetic. She had willed herself to bear the terrible digging and the pain, sure that if she complained the dentist would become angry with her and hurt her more. She had been in the dentist's power as now she was in the power of Carlos and his terrible story.

When Carlos finished she saw him looking at her, trying to see if she believed him. As shocking as the story was she did believe it. With a growing panic she admitted to herself that the dates were accurate. Steve had flown down to the capital from the university to interview the Costa Doran poet, José Iberro. When he returned from the trip he had been incensed for days about the upcoming election in the country. The candidate who was the favorite had a past record of brutality. While the man claimed he had reformed, that he was for democracy, Steve did not believe him. Steve was angry because the man was being supported by the American government.

Sarah had tried to temper Steve's anger. "The other man is a Marxist and a terrorist, isn't he? There would be a revolution and who knows how many would be killed. Isn't our support of the other candidate a case of the lesser of two evils?"

Steve would not be pacified. "Revolution is just what they need down there. What they don't need is someone like my father taking that government's part."

But when Sarah asked what part in the election Dan was playing, Steve would say nothing. But when his boyhood friend, Jorgé, disappeared, Steve could talk of nothing else. "The army has him. They'll murder him, and no one will be able to prove a thing." Then Jean had written them that Jorgé had been freed and Steve seemed so cheered he might himself have been responsible for freeing Jorgé.

Two weeks later Dan was dead. Sarah had thought Steve's depression when he returned from the funeral was regret over his years of criticism of Dan. Now she knew why Steve had left the university, had hidden away like a mortally wounded animal. She tried to catch her breath, to struggle up from the shock. "Why are you telling me this?" she managed, hating having to sit at the same table with Carlos.

A little line of ants had been filing bravely up a leg of the table and across the table's top toward a drop of Coke. Carlos swept them from the table. Suddenly Sarah felt sorry for the ants. "I tell you because of something we wish you to do for us—*una bondad*, a kindness."

"And if I refuse?" She could not imagine doing anything for a man who would tell her such things.

"We have our sources in the American media. It would be easy for us to tell to them the story that I just told to you. It is a sensational one, *si?* It would make good headlines. And I think your husband's mother, Señora Pierce, would not like to read such a story."

Sarah was appalled. To have people pick up a sensational paper and read about Steve, to have Jean hear the ugly story, a story which would make Dan's death into a horror, was unthinkable. "You can't do that. No one would believe it."

"Ah, *Señora*, it is not a struggle to believe the worst of someone. You believe it."

She couldn't hide her belief. As she looked at Carlos she saw greed in his eyes and she began to understand. "You want me to get something for you."

"We want to give you the privilege of doing something for the revolution. You are in a unique position to deliver for us something that belongs to the people. We saw in the paper that the archaeologists at the dig have made a discovery. They will give it to the reactionary Costa Doran government. We want you to get us the warrior they have found. We will sell it and the money will do some good."

Sarah was horrified that her prattling on to the reporter had led to this. Quickly she said, "That's impossible. Even if I could do such a thing the statue would be immediately recognized as stolen. You couldn't possibly sell it."

The waiter, drawn by the evident confrontation, sidled closer to their table. Carlos gave him a withering look and he hastily withdrew to the other side of the café. Turning back to Sarah, Carlos explained with the patience one shows a very young child, "It is not a question of selling it publicly. We know someone who has a private collection. He merely wishes to possess it. There are such men, you know. They are very private in their desires. They have no need to show off their collections. This man would pay well and just now our cause is badly in need of money. You will get the warrior for us and we will keep Steve's sad little story to ourselves."

Sarah could not bear to think of Jean learning the truth. And what would be the university's response? The possibility of Steve's returning to his career there would be gone forever. She considered the children. What would they think of their father when they learned what Steve had done? It was the children that made her begin to think of ways of spiriting the warrior away. After all, it was only an artifact, only a leftover from some ancient civilization, while Steve and Jean and the children were alive and might suffer irreparable harm.

The taking of the warrior would be simple for Sarah because she was trusted. Steve's reputation would be saved. And Jean would never have to know what her son had done.

The warrior, after all, was about to be buried for a second time in an obscure museum where visitors would give it only a fleeting glance. How could a small stone statue, fashioned hundreds of years ago, outweigh the happiness of several human beings? The Maya had a complex way of reckoning time known as the Long Count of Days, with a calendar based on not one year but fifty-two years. Their time seemed to go on forever. What would the Long Count of Days be like for Steve and Jean and the children if she did not protect them?

Watching her Carlos saw her weakening. "You see it would not be too difficult. No one would suspect you." He gave her a crumpled scrap of paper with a number on it. "You can reach me here at any time. The money is needed now. I can give you no more than two days to work out a plan." He signaled to the waiter and requested the check, "*Cuánto?*"

The waiter waved away the idea. "*No, señor, por favor, no se moleste. Permítame.*"

Carlos smiled. "You see," he said to Sarah. "They won't take our money. The people love us."

She had not seen love but only fear on the waiter's face.

Sarah collapsed into the van, too shaken to start back to the digs. Across the street, Carlos drove off in a rusted car. She told herself in taking the warrior she would be able to make it up to Steve for not understanding the agony he had been going through, for not trusting him, for not trying to comfort him. Earlier that day she had even been planning to take the children and leave him.

Sarah began to think how the theft—and she was careful to call it a theft, so as not to deceive herself—might be accomplished. She would have no trouble taking the warrior. She was one of the most trusted members of the digs. In fact, it was she who usually locked the warrior away. The window of the room in which it was kept was barred, but the bars were rusted and might easily be forced, making it appear that someone had broken into the room. The warrior was small. She would have no difficulty hiding it. It would never occur to Professor Reisner to search the rooms of the staff.

Sarah looked around. There were no other cars on the street. No one appeared to be watching her. On an impulse she turned toward the small village where she had lived for five of the happiest years of her childhood. As the road twisted up a series of hills the air became cooler. There were more trees now and in many places the road was shaded. Because the road was so poor it was impossible to travel more than twenty-five miles an hour, but the time passed quickly while she rehearsed over and over her theft of the warrior.

When she reached the village she was shocked at how everything had stayed the same, even after all those years. In the States in just a year's time a shopping mall might cover an empty field, an office tower rise where a small store once stood, a housing development displace a forest. But in this small town nothing had changed. The same tiny stores still displayed their modest wares. One store displayed beans, squash, chili peppers, and a handful of shriveled oranges; another some shelves of pop; another a few dusty lengths of cloth, the folds of the cheap material bleached by the sun. There was the familiar town square with a pack of skinny dogs lying in the sun, probably descendents of the dogs she had once fed scraps saved from her dinner.

In the backyards, chickens scratched in the dust among the rows of corn and the ubiquitous avocado trees. In one yard stood a pile of what looked like logs. Sarah knew the hollowed logs, sealed at each end with plaster, were home to the benevolent, stingless honey bees of Costa Dora.

Maria's house was still there. One difference caught her eye. The house where her own family had lived and where her father had had his clinic was now a café. She remembered the women who had traveled many miles with their babies and children needing her father's help. But her father's clinic had been only a minute remedy in a country where half the babies were dying from malnutrition or disease.

People were beginning to stare at her van. In a moment someone she had known might recognize her. There would be questions. They would want her to stop and visit. How could she face them now, as the missionaries' daughter, when she was plotting a theft that would betray her closest friends? She imagined the expression on Professor Reisner's face when he learned the warrior was missing. Quickly she turned the van around.

As she reached the town where she had met Carlos, in what now seemed a lifetime ago, she saw a ragged procession of Maya coming down the road from a distant village. They were dressed in their best clothes, the men in mismatched black suits. Some of the men had straw hats, others had bright cloths wound around their heads. The women and children trailing behind the men wore blouses and shawls richly embroidered in reds and blues and greens. The little retinue carried the picture of a saint enclosed in a kind of jerry-built cage of sticks to which were tied brightly colored balloons. They were on their way to the village church with an offering of candles and flowers for some happy event or perhaps, Sarah thought, in expiation for some sin committed by a member of the village. For a moment she had a bizarre vision of herself and Jean and the children marching toward the church asking for forgiveness for Steve.

Reluctant to go back to the digs and face Professor Reisner, Sarah found herself getting out of the van and joining the other villagers as they followed the procession. At the steps of the church the procession stopped and one of the young marchers began to set off firecrackers. There was general cheering among the watching children and pleas for more, but evidently the small store was all the group could afford. The procession headed into the church where candles were distributed and one after another fixed to the floor of the church and lighted until the dark church was filled with smoke, the odor of melting wax, and a brilliant light as well.

Sarah slipped into a back row of the church. There was no service going on but it was as busy as a marketplace. It could not have been more unlike the church she and the children attended in Michigan. Her church was all orderliness and circumspection. There were days and evenings when no meeting or service was going on and the church, unlike this one, would be deserted. She tried to imagine her pastor in these primitive celebrations and could not.

She remembered an evening last year when she had stopped at her northern church to drop off food prepared for a funeral luncheon the next day. It was the first time Sarah had seen the church deserted and darkened. For a moment she had been almost afraid, then experienced a selfish exultation in having the church all to herself, as if God would turn from everything else to give her his undivided attention and any problem she had would quickly be solved. It was what she longed for now. In the midst of this busy festivity she longed for the time in the silent, empty church when she had God all to herself.

Driving back to the dig she planned what she must do.

17

Jean stared out at bare trees, their blackness pointed up by an edging of fresh snow. She thought of the old capital of Costa Dora, where the purple and yellow flowers of the jacaranda trees, gaudy as cheap chinaware, would be in bloom.

The school bus materializing through a curtain of snow broke into her musings, surprising her. Red lights flashed on and off as it stopped in front of the cabin. Tim jumped down the high step. But as Jean waited for Mia to follow, the bus door closed, the red lights stopped flashing, and the bus pulled away.

Tim walked toward the cabin, kicking up white gusts of snow with his boots. He held his lunch box in one hand, and in the other a sheet of ivory-colored drawing paper pressed protectively against his chest to shield it from the blowing snow. He hurried in.

"They let us out at noon because it was snowing so hard, but some of the kids said it was because Mr. Peterson wanted to go hunting."

He handed Jean his picture for safekeeping while he pulled off his boots and jacket. The painting was a winter scene of black trees with an overlay of white chalk for the snow. "Your picture is exactly what I've been looking at from the window,

Tim. Where's Mia?"

Tim looked unhappy about having his picture hurried over. "We boiled maple syrup and dropped it in the snow. It was supposed to get hard and make candy but it just stayed melted. We ate it anyhow. Miss Rosier said a bad word when it didn't work."

All the while he was talking Jean noticed that Tim seemed to be looking around for something. Suddenly it occurred to her that Tim was looking for Mia. He must have expected to find her here. Jean felt a chill go through her. "Tim, *where* is Mia?"

"Isn't she here?"

"You can see she isn't." Jean had become impatient.

Tim looked down at the floor. Jean could barely hear his answer. "She didn't go."

"She didn't go to school?"

"No."

Jean was confused. How could you possibly play hooky in the middle of the woods, miles from the nearest village and in a snowstorm? "Where did she go?" Jean could not help alarm creeping into her voice.

"We saw Mr. Crites drive into our woods to shoot a deer. Mia went after him."

"After him?" Jean had heard shots earlier in the morning. She hadn't thought anything about it.

"Dad said he shouldn't shoot on our property. Mia was going to stop him."

"Tim, you're absolutely *sure* Mia didn't get on the bus with you?"

He nodded his head.

"Maybe she got a ride into town with someone?"

Tim appeared impatient at all the questioning. At the same

time he was becoming defensive. "She wasn't *at* school."

"How do you know?"

"They asked me."

"When you told them she didn't get on the bus with you they should have called me immediately." She saw the guilty expression on his face. "Tim, you *did* tell them?"

Tim began to cry.

* * *

Steve was driving the salt truck. The plow, invisible through the snow, was a half mile ahead. He used his phone to keep in touch with Moon Dogett, who was working the plow, and Ted Rainey, the dispatcher at the road commission headquarters. Rainey was furious at having to work on the opening day of the hunting season. "If it weren't for this snowstorm," Rainey complained, "I'd have the day off. They already got two deer hung up on the buck pole in town." Each year the deer taken on opening day were strung along a pole in the center of town. The merchants gave a prize for the largest buck. "Al Roberge has one and Hazen Crites has the other. Both of them good-sized."

Seated in the cab of his truck, Steve wondered if Crites had gotten the deer in his woods. He was glad he had changed his mind about letting Crites hunt there. Steve was very nearly content. He was warm, comfortable, enclosed. A thermos of hot coffee was balanced on the seat beside him. And Rainey had stopped his flow of complaints and hadn't been heard from for some minutes. The radio, tuned to a PBS station, was playing a Brahms trio. Outside the truck, the northwest winds swept the snow across the fields and onto the roads, narrowing them to one barely passable lane. The cello had just begun the darkly colored figure of the final movement of the trio, which suited Steve's mood exactly, when his phone rang. It was Rainey. "Steve, your mother just called. She says you better come home. We'll get someone to take over your truck. It's Al's day off but he's already got his deer. I'll get him in."

Steve's first thought was of Sarah because she was too far away to be under his protection. His mother at home seemed perfectly safe. He had heard the school buses had been sent home early but they were off the roads now and there had been no mention of an accident. He turned the truck around and drove much faster than he should have to the garage. In his haste he forgot to close the tailgate of the truck, and as he sped along, the truck continued to seed the snow with salt.

* * *

Harry responded to Jean's call with amazing speed, arriving at the Pierce home still dressed in his hunting clothes. "I'll go see Crites," Harry said. "You call the sheriff and tell him to meet me at the road into the woods in five minutes." He hugged Jean and left.

The sheriff was matter-of-fact in his questioning and both quick and thorough. "Looks like they missed the boat all the way—the boy, the school. We'll get on it right away. I've got some deputies I can call up. I don't know if you want the media contacted. The exposure might alert anyone who saw her. On the other hand they'll be around you like flies."

* * *

After she hung up Jean noticed Tim hunched up on the couch. He was white-faced with fright. Jean sank down next to him and put her arms around him. He nestled onto her lap and began to cry. After a minute passed he managed, "If Mia's lost for good what'll happen? She always tells me where to go and what to do."

"We'll find her, Tim." Jean tried to reassure him. "Don't blame yourself. It was just a series of misunderstandings. It's no one's fault." In a few minutes he seemed comforted and they stood together at the window watching for Steve.

At last his truck pulled up and Steve came running up to the door. Jean met him, and in spite of the calm recitation she had been rehearsing, she blurted out the facts.

He was trembling with anger. "I'm going over there and beat the truth out of Crites."

Jean was alarmed at his fury. Quickly she said, "Harry's already there, Steve," but before she could finish, Steve was out the door. She looked at Tim. He was mindlessly tearing up his painting into narrow strips. He had no idea what he was doing and Jean did not have the heart to bring it to his attention. She sat down and, putting her arm around him, began to wait. All her childhood prayers crowded into her mind and she began to try one and then another.

18

Harry Wachner pulled onto the narrow two-track that led to the Crites' shack. Without taking time to slam the pickup door behind him, Harry covered the walk in a few strides. Lights were on and he heard movements, but no one answered his knock. He tried the handle but the door was locked. "Crites," he shouted, "open this door." There was a brief wait and then the door was pulled open a grudging inch or two.

Grimly Harry forced his way into the house. A startled Crites hastily retreated from the door. His wife stood by a table covered with dirty lunch dishes. The room was too hot, and the space heater gave off a gassy smell that sickened Harry. The shack was a graveyard of ugly objects. Harry had often seen Crites' car at local garage sales and suspected Edna Crites of taking in discarded furnishings the way that some people take in derelict cats or dogs. In the face of such uncontrolled need his anger dwindled, but then he saw a deer rifle leaning against a chair. Fear for Mia made his anger flare up.

"Crites, we know you drove into the trail in Pierce's woods this morning. Both the Pierce children saw you, and the girl went in after you to tell you that you had no business hunting there. No one's seen her since. We think she's still in the woods. You tell me what you know or tell it to the sheriff—at the county jail."

Crites tried to look past Harry as though searching for witnesses who would come forward to support him. "Why come to me? I haven't seen her. I got my deer in Pierce's woods all right, but as soon as I dressed it out, I took it to town and then I come right home. When I got home my wife said Pierce's mother called and said it was all right for me to hunt there. I don't see I did anything wrong."

"He was back here just as *Sally Jessy* came on," his wife said.

Harry insisted, "You couldn't have gone in and out of there without seeing that child. Her brother said she followed you in."

"I never seen her. I was looking for my buck."

"Crites, if you're lying and anything has happened to that child in this storm, I'll see that you end up behind bars."

Crites looked nervously around. "There's no need to threaten me, Harry. There's lots of people out there in the woods besides me. What about those crazy Valhallists? They do plenty of shooting in the woods—and not for deer either."

"They're miles away and you know it. You're the one she went after, Crites. Look at that snow out there. Every minute counts."

Crites shrugged. "Let's go. I'll give you a hand looking for her. Not because I know anything about where she is but I know those woods backwards and forwards."

* * *

Crites sat silently as Harry headed his pickup into the snow-storm. Crites was trying to decide what direction to take when they got to the woods, and to imagine what the girl could tell on him when they found her. He decided she wouldn't know anything and he'd be safe to lead them in the direction where he had last seen her. But suppose that's where they found her? Wouldn't that make them suspicious of him? They would wonder how he knew to go in just that direction. Maybe he should head them in another direction first and then gradually work around that way. Still, he didn't like to think of her—of any-one—out alone in this weather. She had been so good at sneaking around after him in the woods all summer, it had never occurred to him that she would have trouble finding her way home.

One of the sheriff's deputies was waiting for them at the entrance to the Pierce property. The deputy's car door was open so he could hear his radio. Next to the deputy's car was Steve Pierce's truck. Crites saw with relief it was empty and that for the moment he would not have to face Pierce.

The deputy said, "Harry, the sheriff took a couple of the deputies and Pierce and they divided up. I can reach them over this." He held up his phone.

"Tell them I've got Crites here," Harry said. "He says he doesn't know where the girl is but he'll help us." With a sinking heart Crites heard the skepticism in Harry's voice. He knew Harry didn't believe him and would be watching everything he did with suspicion.

The sky behind the black trees was darkening. As they entered the woods Harry said, "There may not be much the law can do about this, Crites, but I'll tell you something. If anything happens to his girl, Pierce will come after you. Maybe you think he's only some college professor who's run away from the city, but I'm telling you, Pierce is a man who's angry enough to do anything."

Crites realized this was true. He began to feel consequences after him like a pack of hungry dogs.

* * *

Mia knew she was lost. But she told herself that Tim would let the school know where she was and the school would call home. It might take time. She realized things adults did always took more time than seemed necessary. Right now she was cold.

She recalled a chapter in her *Woodsman's Guide* that told how to build shelters from boughs. As she headed for some hemlock trees she tried walking backward against the wind, but walking backward didn't work; there were too many things to trip over in the woods. When she came to the trees she began tearing off the branches. Her hands inside her snow-caked mittens were numb with cold and it was hard getting them to do what she wanted. A single branch took several minutes to pry loose and she could manage only the smaller ones. But soon the work warmed her and her hands were no longer numb. From time to time she paused to rest, but never for very long. She had a sense that she must outrun something, but she was not certain what that something was.

When she finally managed to accumulate a pile of branches, Mia started leaning them against a tree and then against one another. Finally she had built up a green tangle of limbs around a small hollow into which she climbed. There were spaces between the branches and she was able to peer out at the place where she had been before. After her movements caused the fretwork to collapse so that it had to be constructed all over again, she learned to remain perfectly still. She was proud of having made her own shelter.

After she had been there for what seemed like hours, Mr. Wachner's three owls appeared out of the twilight and settled with squealing, humming noises onto a tree near her and began to watch for prey—a rabbit or a vole scurrying through the snow. Watching with them she breathed softly and tried not to move. It seemed important that the owls be successful. But no small animal ventured out in the snowstorm. After a long while the owls, one by one, flew off. All the while they were there, she was not afraid. But now that they were gone she began to cry. The last thought she had before drifting into a chilled sleep was of her grandmother abandoned in the berry patch as night fell. Mia thought that she must have felt like she herself now felt—alone and frightened. Mia wished she could tell her grandmother how sorry she was.

Mia awoke, colder than she had ever been in her life, to hear loud movements in the woods. Silently she waited to see if it might be a bear. Only when she heard Mr. Wachner's voice did she call out. She hoped her father was with Mr. Wachner though for some reason that was not clear to her, Mia felt her father was responsible for what had happened to her—for forcing her to build her own shelter. Suddenly it was her father who pushed away the branches and reached for her, picking her up in his arms, holding her more tightly than she had ever been held. Mia tried not to cry; *crying is for babies,* she thought. But when her father's shoulders began to shake with sobs, Mia decided it was all right and, besides, she was already crying.

19

Jean left the window only long enough to give Tim some hot chocolate and put him to bed for a nap. He took his entire menagerie of stuffed animals into bed with him and wouldn't agree to be left alone until Jean promised to wake him as soon as Mia got home. He fell asleep almost instantly.

As the snow piled higher and higher Jean imagined its weight falling on her until she felt it was more than she could bear. The sky grew darker and it was becoming difficult to make out the trees in the distance. Then she thought she saw the beam of a flashlight in the woods. If she had not had to watch over Tim she would have hurried into the woods herself. With a shudder she wondered, *How will I ever explain to Sarah that I failed to protect Mia?*

Bright headlights cut through the darkness, startling her. She counted three cars. The sheriff's car was first to pull up in front of the cabin, then Harry's pickup, and then Steve's truck in the rear. After a minute the sheriff drove away and Harry and Steve came up the walk. Steve was carrying Mia wrapped in a blanket.

Jean flung open the door to the cabin. Mia stirred at the sight of her grandmother, reaching out for her. Reluctantly

Steve let Mia go and Jean pulled the girl to her and held her. When at last Mia stopped crying, Jean remembered that she'd promised to wake Tim.

But Tim was already awake and standing by the door. He was staring at Mia. "I didn't tell on you," he said, "not until after school. I had to tell then because you were gone so long." He looked as though he were waiting for Mia to reproach him.

"It's OK," Mia replied in a weak voice.

Tim continued to look at Mia as though he could not quite believe this was the same Mia who had so often commanded him.

Harry took off his jacket. "I'll make some coffee. I suspect Mia would like some hot chocolate."

Tim asked, "Can I have some, too, even if I wasn't lost?"

Jean put Mia into dry clothes and, settling her on the couch with a blanket, followed Harry to the kitchen. As soon as they were alone Harry put his arms around her. For the first time that day Jean wept. After a minute she pulled away, self-consciously wiping her eyes. "Why is it we always cry when it's over? Relief, I suppose. I wonder if we shouldn't have Dr. Brady look at Mia?"

"Mia is going to be fine. That girl is tough. It's Steve you should worry about. I thought he was going to tear Crites apart. I've been wanting to tell you this for a long time but I didn't want to intrude: Something is going on with Steve. Sarah talked to me about it a couple of times."

"I know," Jean said, as she began to fill the teakettle. "But if I try to question him, it only seems to make it worse."

When she brought in the tray of coffee and cocoa Jean stole a glance at Steve. She had been so relieved to have Mia safe she had paid little attention to him, but now she caught her breath. Harry was right. Steve's face was paper white, his eyes ringed with dark circles. He looked like a man about to commit an act of terrorism—or self-destruction. Jean was so taken aback she could only stand there holding the tray. Quietly Harry took it from her and distributed the cups.

As soon as the coffee and cocoa were consumed Harry excused himself. "I've got to get back to the office or there won't be a paper this week. I'm personally going to write the story about Mia's rescue. Maybe I'll send a photographer out to take your picture, Mia. How would you like that?"

Mia looked pleased. "I can show it to the kids at school."

Steve's head snapped up. "I don't want any photographers around here."

Harry and Jean were silent. Disappointed, Mia said, "That's not fair. Why can't they take my picture?"

"I just don't want them here. That's reason enough."

"I think we're all tired," Harry said. "It's been a long day and a tough one." He exchanged a look with Jean. "Call you in the morning."

* * *

When both children had been fed their dinner and put to bed, Jean sat down across from Steve. He had refused dinner and had not moved from the chair. He was still wearing his down jacket. Gently Jean tried to reassure him. "Steve, it's over. Mia is fine. It might have been much worse." She sighed. "I wonder why people say things like that. To frighten themselves? For comfort?" She looked at Steve.

"To warn themselves," he said. His voice was hoarse, tentative, as though he had not used it in a long time. "I don't know how many more warnings I need to leave this place. When Dad was killed, all I wanted was to get away. I thought I could turn my back and shut out the whole savage world, but it's no safer for my children here than it was at the university—or the countries where I grew up."

Jean reached over to touch his sleeve. "Steve, be honest with me. It's time you told me the truth. That isn't all you were trying to get away from, was it?"

"No, it wasn't. You remember when I came down to Costa Dora a few weeks before Dad died to interview José Ibarro? Something happened while I was down there. When I heard Jorgé had been arrested I was furious, desperate to do something about it. Dad said to leave it to him, but I didn't trust him. I was full of self-importance and I believed I could do something myself. In spite of Dad's warning I contacted one of the guerrillas, proud of knowing one of the leaders. He was called Carlos, though I doubt that is his real name." Jean was staring at him but he could not look at her.

"Carlos said there was a rumor that the United States was involved with Costa Dora's military school where their security forces were trained. The Costa Doran government wanted that kept secret at all costs. If I could get some proof that that was so, Carlos would use the information to blackmail the government into letting Jorgé go." Steve buried his head in his hands.

More than anything Jean wanted to stop him, to keep him from saying anything more, but she forced herself to keep silent.

Steve rushed on, his words so long held back, tumbling over one another. "I was convinced Dad would do nothing for

Jorgé—it might embarrass the embassy. I wanted to prove that I had as much power as Dad. That night I waited until you and Dad were asleep and took Dad's keys from the dresser just inside your door. Then I went down to his study and unlocked his files. It was right there in a file, the amount of money the United States was giving to the school. I copied the document, locked the files, and returned the keys."

Jean was paralyzed with anger. She did not think she could bear to hear more, still he went on.

"The next day I gave the incriminating paper to Carlos and flew back to the university. He assured me the paper would save Jorgé. It never occurred to me they would use it to go after Dad. A week later you wrote to say that Jorgé had been freed. By then I had begun to have second thoughts about what I had done but I told myself Jorgé's life was worth a piece of paper.

"When I came down for the funeral you showed me Dad's watch and wallet to let me know it had not been a simple robbery. Of course you had no idea of my part in it. You also showed me the lighter. I knew it belonged to Carlos. I had seen him use it often enough. He'd left it on purpose. He knew eventually I would see it." Steve hid his face in his hands. "I knew what I had done."

"Steve, oh, Steve." So much a nightmare did the story seem that Jean found herself reaching out to touch Steve's arm to assure herself it was all real.

In a choked voice Steve went on, "Then Jorgé walked into the house. 'To pay respects to your father,' he said. It was like seeing someone back from the dead. Jorgé took me aside and told me Dad had arranged with the government to have him freed. Dad stuck his neck out to save Jorgé's life. I tried to tell him he was mistaken, that it had been Carlos who had saved him. He laughed bitterly. 'Saved me?' he said. 'It was Carlos who betrayed me to the government soldiers. I could never figure out why. But it was your dad that got me out.'"

Jean was staring at Steve but he could not look at her.

"It was then that I saw what I had done. Carlos had betrayed Jorgé to get me to betray my father. I saw that I had killed my own father. I keep having a nightmare that just before they shot Dad, he thought, 'Those are Steve's people.'" Steve began to cry.

Jean realized she had not seen Steve cry as a child. He was always so self-contained. She reached across the table and took Steve's hands and held them to her own wet cheeks. *How terrible our secrets grow when we keep them from one another!* she thought. Like plants growing in darkness, stunted, deformed, ugly things.

She promised herself that Steve would never guess the effort it cost her to continue to clasp his hands. Somehow she managed to find words. "We can't know how or why it happened, Steve. But your father knew that in a country like Costa Dora his job was a dangerous one. If you hadn't revealed that information it would certainly have come out sooner or later. You can't be responsible for the evil things people do." Jean tried to make her voice convincing, to hide the shock and the anger she felt. *But Dan is dead,* she thought. *Nothing can bring him back, but Steve is still here.* He could still be saved if she could just convince him that he was forgiven so that he might forgive himself.

Abruptly Steve got up and headed for the door.

Alarmed, Jean stopped him. "Where are you going?"

"Don't worry. I'm not going to do anything foolish. I just want to clear my head. You turn in. I'll close up when I get back." He saw her worried look. "Honestly, I'm all right."

Somehow Jean believed Steve. Wearily she nodded and headed down the hall. She shut her bedroom door behind her and, too tired to undress, kicked off her shoes and pulled the blanket over her as if she might hide under it. Although she was more exhausted than she had ever remembered being she felt as if she would never sleep again. She could not stop herself from going over and over Steve's story. She knew Steve so well she could understand what had made him betray his father. The ironic part was that he had inherited his passion for fairness from Dan. The same dedication to justice that had fueled Steve's reckless association with the guerrillas was the very thing that had sustained Dan all those years in his work for the foreign office. They had been like two men walking the same path, invisible to one another. How had she failed to help Dan and Steve see this and to see it herself?

As the long night moved toward dawn and the moon arced across the sky becoming visible through her window just as it was setting, Jean found she could forgive Steve just as she could forgive herself. What she had heard that evening from Steve had helped her to see what forgiveness was—wholehearted or not at all.

* * *

Steve found the silence of the snow-covered woods restful. The moon laid striped shadows across the white ground. In a nearby tree Harry's three owls sat motionless staring down at him as if they were going to pronounce judgment. He felt he had been on a long journey, a journey traveled without rest, and worse, without direction. He did not think he would ever forgive himself. However much his mother loved him, she might never forgive him. If he were to go on with his life he would have to find forgiveness somewhere. Only Sarah and her God could give him that, and Sarah was a thousand miles away and her God with her.

20

It was an exhausting day at the dig. Unbearable heat alternated with steamy showers. The rain ate away at an area they had carefully excavated, causing it to cave in and make an extra week's work for everyone. Later the staff ate its way solemnly through dinner. There were none of the usual jokes and good-natured jibes. After a halfhearted hand of bridge between Sarah and Ernesto, and two of the associates, there was a general decision to turn in. Sarah locked the warrior up and went to her room.

She waited until midnight before making her way to the room where the warrior was kept. In the pocket of her robe were a pair of gloves and a screwdriver. She decided that if anyone asked what she was doing she could simply say she had forgotten whether she had locked the room. Although the room was dark she knew it well enough to find her way about. The window was a slightly lighter square in the darkness around her. She put on her gloves and, placing the screwdriver between the sill and the window, forced the lock so that the window swung open. In a moment the warrior was clutched in her hands. She couldn't see it but she knew its shape by heart.

The warrior seemed to move in her grasp. She told herself it was only her quick breathing and the trembling of her hands.

All the justifications for taking the warrior flashed through her mind. She had believed she could do anything to protect Steve and Jean and the children, but now she recalled a conversation years before when Steve had taken her to visit the guerrillas. She had argued with Steve that violence by the government did not justify violence on the part of the guerrillas. Back then she had been contemptuous of Steve's argument that the ends justify the means. Now she asked herself if that wasn't exactly the excuse she was using.

Her parents seemed to have crowded into the tiny room with her. She couldn't help but wonder what they would think if they could see her now. Sarah had never been able to hold her own in arguments with Steve over religion. She was familiar with all the theories against religion he presented so glibly. And though she knew he was wrong, her own faith was not much different than it had been when she was ten. Maybe if she had read more books she would know what to do. Now she asked herself, *If I were in trouble, would I want Steve to steal for me? Even to save me from embarrassment and misery?* She returned the warrior to its box and quietly locked the door behind her.

In the morning she hurried to Dr. Reisner. "You had better come and see! The window in the locked room has been forced open. Fortunately the warrior is safe. I think we ought to take the warrior into the city and have it locked up."

A pale Dr. Reisner agreed. "I'll take it myself. Today." He wiped perspiration from his forehead. "A narrow escape. I would never have forgiven myself if something had happened to it."

Sarah did not want to meet Carlos again but when she called the number he had given her, a man told her Carlos was "unavailable." *"Uno momento,"* he said. Sarah waited impatiently, her hand clutching the receiver, damp with sweat. After what seemed an eternity the same voice ordered, "Carlos says 'At the same café. *Mañana.* Four o'clock.'" With that he hung up.

Now she sat with Carlos across from her. "I can't do it," she said. "Anyhow it's too late. The statue was taken away today and locked up. I know Steve wouldn't have wanted me to steal it, whatever he has to face. But, Carlos, he was on your side. He was your friend. How can you betray a friend?"

Carlos scowled at her. "In times of life and death, friendship is a bourgeois extravagance. We are desperate for money." He stared at her. His voice grew almost pleasant but Sarah did not trust it. "I guessed when you called you would not do as we asked. Very well. But the decision of what to do about Steve is not mine. The decision will be made by a man who is waiting outside in my car. Perhaps you can convince him to keep quiet." He emptied what was left in his can of Coke—downing it in one quick swallow—and stood up, tossing some coins on the table.

Sarah hesitated. She didn't trust him but she couldn't afford to lose any opportunity of stopping Steve's exposure. Before they left the café Carlos walked over to the counter and leaning across it spoke rapidly to the proprietor. The man stiffened, a look of pure fright on his face. He nodded several times. Carlos returned and led Sarah out of the door. The car, an ancient station wagon, was parked on a deserted street. There were two men in the wagon, one in the back and one in the driver's seat.

"We will attract attention standing here," Carlos said, motioning her to get into the back seat. "He is the man to talk to. Perhaps you will have some luck."

There was a rapacity on Carlos's face that made Sarah panic. She looked quickly at the empty street, ready to run. Carlos grabbed her arm and as the wagon door opened pushed her into the car. The man inside put a gun to her head. "Be quiet," he hissed. Carlos was beside her. He tore off a piece of duct tape and sealed her mouth. Then he slipped a blindfold over her eyes. Rope bound her wrists and ankles. As she was pushed to the floor of the car Carlos said, "You are an ambassador's daughter-in-law. Let us see if you are worth as much as an old statue."

Sarah clenched her hands and tensed her body to stop her trembling. The air on the floor of the car was thick with fumes from exhaust seeping up through the car's floor. *I have to think, to use my head,* she told herself. She began to count seconds and minutes so she would have some idea of how far she was taken. The road was a rough one and her body bounced against the floor of the car. The man in the back seat started to say something in Spanish but Carlos stopped him. "She speaks Spanish," he said. After that there were only whispers and silence.

When the car stopped Sarah was unsure of how much time had passed. In her terror she had lost count, but she thought they had been traveling for an hour on these roads that would have meant no more than thirty or forty miles. Every bone in her body ached. Her throat was parched from the smoke and fumes. A man lifted her from the car and hustled her into some sort of shelter. Sarah guessed it was a house or shack of some kind.

She was pushed roughly and then she heard a door slam behind her. "Here are the rules," Carlos said. "I will remove the tape and the ropes from your legs and your blindfold, but if you make a sound they go back on. There will be two men in the room next door. If you try to escape their orders are to shoot. Do you understand?"

Sarah nodded. Carlos was careless, or worse, cruel, in cutting the rope that bound her legs, for the knife scratched Sarah and left a trickle of blood. He slammed the door as he left her. She was glad he was gone so that he could not see the tears she was unable to hold back. The room was empty of any furniture. She sank down onto the dirt floor. How long would it take people at the dig to realize she was gone? Who would they call? The local police who might be involved with the guerrillas, or the army that had its own political agenda which would have nothing to do with her safety? Would they call Steve? And what would Steve tell the children? Who would pay her ransom? Steve had no money and Jean had nothing more than her pension and a little in savings. If money wasn't found would they kill her?

She told herself she had to keep a clear head, to be methodical and rational. It was her only chance. She forced herself to examine the tiny room. Boards had been nailed across the one window. The floor was dirt, the ceiling corrugated metal, the walls adobe.

It seemed hours but it might have been only minutes when a man entered the room, his face covered by a knitted mask. He handed her a *chuchito* and a can of orange pop. She considered refusing to eat but she knew that if she didn't keep her strength up any opportunity to escape would be wasted. Awkwardly she managed the food with her bound hands. He went out of the room for a moment to return with a pail. "Toilet," the man said and left her, locking the door after himself. When she was alone she noticed the discarded tab from the can of pop. She managed to pick it up and carefully worked it into the dirt floor of the shack.

As the room darkened Sarah heard voices in the next room. Standing next to the door, she made out two men talking. They were not speaking Spanish. She pressed her ear against the door. She was shocked to hear them speaking the Mayan language that was used in the countryside of her childhood village. Of course they would never have guessed she knew even a word of a Mayan language, much less the very one they were speaking, a language used in only a small section of Costa Dora. Immediately another thought occurred to her. Could those men be from her village, perhaps even someone she knew?

As she listened to the men, slowly the Mayan words came back to her. But it was no secret conversation she was listening to that would tell her what her fate was to be. The men were discussing a soccer game in great detail. It seemed barbaric for them to sit outside of a room where a human being was in terror and chat about some game.

She tried to recall from books and newspaper articles what prisoners did, for she had no preparation. There were no courses in school, no guides handed down from friends or parents. She felt as if she was the first person in the world to whom this had happened. She thought of Maria's father who had been taken away by the government forces. He had been on the side of the guerrillas. On Carlos' side. Sarah could not sort things out.

There was no need to devise a prayer. Her whole body and mind was one shriek to heaven for deliverance, a plea for angels to come down as they had come down to protect Daniel in the lions' den. But as the hours passed and darkness shut out even the sliver of light that had squeezed through the cracks in the boarded window, no angels made their way through the corrugated roof.

21

Steve came in out of the cold night and knew he would not be able to sleep. Wondering if he would ever sleep again, he settled into a chair. The chilled and darkened room with its dying fire suited Steve. Before his confession to his mother, it was somehow possible to believe his betrayal of his father was an aberration, a nightmare he had made up. It was even possible to believe for minutes at a time that it had never happened. But with his confession the terrible event had taken on a life of its own and could never be denied. He did not see how he could live with it, how he could face his mother each day—or himself.

He went to check on Mia. She was sound asleep, her hair spread over her pillow, and her favorite doll, whom she insisted she no longer played with, lay beside her. In Steve's own room Tim was barely visible among the menagerie of stuffed animals sharing his bed. Steve was envious of his children's ability to find comfort so easily.

Back in the living room, Steve dropped off to sleep in the chair but was awakened by the ringing of the phone. It was still dark outside and the fire had died out. Confused, Steve looked at his watch. Six in the morning. He picked up the receiver expecting to hear the road crew dispatcher, Ted Rainy, telling him he was needed on the morning crew. Instead, an official-sounding woman's voice asked if the person speaking was Stephen Pierce. "Yes, this is Stephen Pierce."

"Please hold for the American ambassador in Costa Dora." There was a brief silence. At first Steve thought it was a cruel joke. "But the ambassador is dead," he wanted to say. Then he remembered that Jim Benkin had taken his father's place. Steve wondered if somehow they had learned at the embassy that he was responsible for what had happened to his father.

"Steve," a familiar voice came on the line. "This is Jim Benkin. I'm sorry, but I have to be brief. You're going to be getting a call shortly from State. Since I've known your family for a long time I thought I'd better to tell you myself."

"Tell me what?"

"I'm afraid it's a little worrisome. Actually, Sarah is missing."

Steve held the receiver as though it were struggling to get away. "What do you mean, missing?" he asked in a hoarse voice.

"She left the dig in a van yesterday afternoon. She didn't return. We located the van but there was no sign of her. Late last night we got a note from a rebel guerrilla group saying she was being held by them. They're demanding a ransom."

Steve could barely hold on to the phone. "Is she all right?"

"Yes. The note assures us she is fine."

"Then we'll pay the ransom. I'll send it right away. How much do they want?"

"I'm afraid they want a million dollars."

Steve was stunned. "I'm sure I could scrape together something, but a million dollars? Will the State Department help?"

"I'm sorry, but you must know that the government has a policy of not paying ransom. We're doing everything we can to find her but you understand what the conditions are down here." Steve heard a note of disapproval in Benkin's voice. Steve realized Benkin must have known about his involvement with the guerrillas. Steve winced. *He thinks I deserve this.*

"Steve," Benkin was saying, "I'd strongly advise against your attempting to pay them anything. How do we know they wouldn't just take the money and do away with Sarah? And you know it would set a bad precedent."

"Precedent! What do I care about precedents! We're talking about Sarah."

"Of course it's up to you, but as you say the sum is impossible. I just wanted you to know how sorry we are about this and that we are doing everything under the sun to find Sarah."

"I'll get the next flight down," Steve said.

There was a pause on the line and for a minute Steve thought they had been disconnected.

"I wouldn't do that."

"Why not?" Steve was stunned.

"I'm afraid I'm going to have to be brutally honest with you, Steve. Sarah's life may depend on your staying away. Some of us at the embassy knew of your sympathy toward the guerrillas. Of course we realized that they had a lot of right on their side—no one could condone what past governments down here have done—but frankly your meetings with guerrilla supporters made us more than a little uncomfortable. To protect your father's feelings we didn't say anything. But the Costa Dora government knew. If you come down now it will complicate things for the government. They are trying to keep things quiet. And whatever you may think of them, believe me, they are doing everything they can to get Sarah back. The last thing they want is an international incident that will turn Americans against Costa Dora. Do us all a favor, Steve, and stay where you are. We'll be in touch as soon as we hear anything." There was a click on the otherend of the line but Steve, desperate to keep a connection to Costa Dora, could not hang up. It was only when Jean, sleepy-eyed and in her robe, came into the room that he replaced the receiver.

"I heard the phone ring. Steve, what is it? You're as pale as a ghost. Mia is safe, there's nothing to worry about now."

"Not only was I responsible for Dad's death and Mia nearly freezing to death, now I've lost Sarah." Steve sank down on a chair, his hands hiding his face, his shoulders shaking with sobs.

Jean knelt beside him, her hand on his arm. "Steve, tell me what's happened."

"Sarah has been kidnapped by the guerrillas. They're holding her for ransom."

Jean stared at Steve. "Are you sure? Who called?"

"Jim Benkin." They both knew Benkin was a man who would never make a claim that was not supported by facts.

Jean drew her robe more closely around her to shut out the chill of the room and the chill of the world. "Steve, if it's money they want, we'll find it. I can draw out my pension. There's my house in the old capital."

"Mother," Steve groaned, "they want a million dollars."

"That seems an impossible amount but I have friends, and there's my sister and brother. I know they would help. What about the State Department?"

Steve shook his head. "You know what their policy is: no ransoms. I feel so helpless. I wanted to go down but they don't want me there. They think it would complicate things, maybe endanger Sarah."

"I could go down, Steve."

"No. If this gets out and hits the papers and television there will be no way we can keep the children from hearing about it. They'll need you here."

The phone rang again. Steve grabbed it. A formal voice identified herself as calling from the State Department. "I'm afraid," she said, "We have some worrisome news." Steve winced at the word "worrisome." Did everyone from the State Department read from the same script? Did they give out certain words each morning?

In a hoarse voice he said, "I know what's happened. What I want to know is, what are you going to do about it?"

* * *

After the children left for school Steve stayed by the phone while Jean made the hour's drive to a town where she could find a copy of the *New York Times*. She and Steve scanned the paper but there was no mention of the kidnapping. They listened to every television and radio newscast. So far the State Department had managed to keep things quiet. Steve called Costa Dora several times until Benkin no longer came to the phone but had his secretary, Evelyn Seburn, talk with Steve. "I'm so sorry, Steve," she said. "Honestly, if you were here you could see we're doing everything possible to find your wife. We all just feel terrible. We're praying for Sarah. You call anytime. I'll be right here. And give my love to your mother."

It was the first understanding voice Steve had heard over the

phone and it was too much for him. He could cope with for-
mality and indifference but how was he to endure love? He
rushed out of the house, slamming the door behind him.

22

Sarah made a mark on the dirt floor each day she was held. That there were only three marks seemed incredible to her, for it seemed as though she had been there forever. She could hardly remember what the rest of her life was like. She would have given anything to be back with Steve in those cold, bare woods, even with his moods. All that was nothing compared with her imprisonment, which could very well be only a prelude to death. There was nothing in the room to divert her, only the constant chatter in the other room of the two men who were guarding her. She felt as though she were inhabiting the Mayan underworld, the place the Maya believed the sun and moon went after they had disappeared below the horizon.

She divided her days. She did not sleep during the day, for if she did, she knew she would not sleep at night and the night went on forever. Each morning she tried to ease her chafed wrists as she recited to herself all of the Bible verses she recalled from her Sunday school days. MKs were expected to excel in knowledge of Scripture, and as a dutiful child she had memorized more than she was assigned. Now it was a resource. The Psalms had always been her favorite.

... thou hast known my soul in adversities; and hast not shut me up into the hand of the enemy: thou has set my feet in a large room....

... I am feeble and sore broken: I have roared by reason of the disquietness of my heart. Lord, all my desire is before thee; and my groaning is not hid from thee.

Sarah's father always insisted on the King James Bible. "Magnificent language for magnificent words," he had said, and for long minutes the soaring language carried her out of her prison.

After going over the verses she allowed herself a time to think of Mia and Tim and Steve. But that was so painful she could hardly bear it. There was a period of time given to thinking over the paper she had planned to write under Dr. Reisner's supervision on the dig. In the afternoon she allowed herself to recall some time when she had been happy. At first she imagined times like the day of her marriage to Steve or the first day she had taught a class at the university or the time she and her roommate at the university had taken a trip to Europe, but the extraordinary was not what she wanted. What she needed was the ordinary: dinners around the kitchen table with Steve and the children, walks in the woods with Mia and Tim, evenings in front of the fire reading with Steve. The more exotic memories seemed unreachable in these surroundings, but the simple ones she could lay a hand on.

Carlos had not returned. Twice a day a hooded man came into her room with food, which she managed as best she could with her hands bound at the wrists. He would not answer her questions; he would not speak to her at all. It was this sullen silence in him that started her wondering. It seemed so at odds with the cheerful arguing over the soccer game she heard in the other room. It was hard to believe it was the same man.

That evening she listened again at the door. The words were familiar. The whole conversation was familiar. Startled she realized the two men were discussing the same game in exactly the same words as they had the evening before, as though it were a recording.

And then she understood: *it was a recording.* Believing she could not understand the Mayan language they simply played a tape over and over, leading her to think what? Of course, that two men were guarding her when all the time there might be only one man or—was it possible?—no one at all. Perhaps this was their guarantee of safety. If the hiding place were tracked down there would be no one there to apprehend. Twice a day a man came to give her the food and then quickly depart. But what of the rest of the time?

Hastily she dug out the metal tabs she had been saving from the pop cans. After a few tries she managed to grasp one in her hands and rub it against the rope that bound her wrists. Over and over it slipped out of her grasp and she had to start again. It seemed to take forever for the first fraying to show. She did not know when the recorded voices might be replaced by a guard, or if that sullen man was still there after all. If he were and if he caught her trying to cut her ropes she might not be given a second chance. They would bind her legs and blindfold her. Or worse.

The first tab bent into a useless shape with her efforts and she dug up a second tab, wasting valuable minutes. The second tab seemed sharper, or maybe the rope was already worn. Her wrist ached from its twisted position, her fingers numb and cramped. Still she worked at the rope, holding her breath as one fiber after another broke apart until finally the rope fell away. Her hands were hers again.

She stopped at the door, unable to summon the courage to open it, unsure of what would be on the other side. Perhaps the voice recording was only a gimmick to allow the guard to sleep in peace. If she opened the door to the other room the guard would awaken and shoot her. Or if he did not shoot her she would surely be bound and blindfolded. There would be no further chance for escape. Quietly she tried the door knowing all along it would be locked. The window! She attempted to pry the boards loose but they were nailed tightly shut. But at least the noise of what she was doing did not bring in a guard.

Frustrated, she sat down in the middle of the room and looked up, admonishing God for bringing her this close to freedom and then deserting her. No solution appeared from on high. There was only the rusty corrugated tin roof. Then she remembered something from her childhood: a rainstorm and her mother complaining of a leaking roof. Her father had taken a ladder, climbed onto the roof, and rearranged the sheets of tin to keep out the water, then replaced the stones that held the sheets down.

The roof was low, but Sarah couldn't reach it. Gritting her teeth, she dumped the contents of the pail and turned it upside down next to the wall. By standing on the pail she could reach the ceiling. The sheets of tin were loose beneath the scattered rocks. She pushed one aside to see the night sky and above her the Southern Cross. The cross seemed a sign. She was sure this would be her way out. The mud walls were not high, perhaps six feet. Standing on the pail she could reach to the top of them but she was not strong enough to lift herself up and over them. Again she listened at the door. The same familiar voices were engaged in an argument over whether the goalkeeper had run with the ball.

Desperately Sarah hunted for one of the discarded tabs and, finding it, she began to dig at the mud wall until she had a niche that would provide a toehold. It was slow, tedious work and used up two precious tabs. But desperation and her training as an archaeologist used to tedious work sustained her. Little by little the mud from the wall crumbled and sifted down to make a small pile. The cavity deepened. She stood on the pail and put her foot into the hollow she had made and pushed herself up, reaching for the top of the wall. She told herself it was like chinning herself in gym class, a class she had always hated. Now she berated herself for not being in better shape. Her arms ached from the weight of her body. She looked again at the open sky and swung herself up. This time she found herself perched on the top of the wall. It took a minute to get up her courage. Gritting her teeth, she let herself drop to the ground, twisting her ankle so that when she walked a sharp stab shot up her leg, but in her hurry to get away she hardly noticed the pain.

She looked around; there was no car. Holding her breath she risked looking into the window of the room that adjoined her prison. By the light of the moon she could just make out a room empty except for a chair, some discarded cans and bottles, and what looked like a tape recorder. But someone could return at any moment. Where should she go? The road would be too dangerous. There was no traffic, but even if a car did come along there would be no way of knowing if the person she flagged down was one of her captors. She turned away from the road, running as fast as she could on her injured ankle, not knowing how soon they would discover her escape and set out after her.

The trunks of the mahogany trees were like dark stripes against the lesser dark of the night. She stumbled over brush and rocks, scraping her knees and bruising her feet. Once she just missed stepping on a snake and realized it was one that her parents had often warned her against. Thinking of her parents' care made her feel how unprotected she now was and brought tears to her eyes. Suddenly she saw a great hill rising up before her. She could not keep herself from wasting the precious moments it took to stop to look at it. She was sure it was a Mayan temple or palace of some kind long since overgrown with grasses and trees. At least someone had been here before her, if only a thousand years ago.

Her ankle ached from the running and she winced at each step. Abruptly she stopped. In front of her was a *cenote,* a sinkhole filled with water. There were many of them in Costa Dora. But this one was strangely familiar. As she knelt to splash water on her face and to drink she almost recognized the taste of the water. On the opposite shore was a sapodilla tree with a grotesquely shaped branch that reached out over the water like an arm. She remembered the tree from her childhood. When Maria was not off picking coffee she would slip away from her weaving and the two of them would hurry to the *cenote* for a swim. They used to hang from the tree and drop into the water.

Sarah began to run toward what was now a known place. She tried to remember how long it had taken them to make the trip from the village to their swimming hole. Twenty minutes. No more. She quickened her pace, not thinking of what she would do when she got to the village, only about getting there.

Long before she reached the village the dogs began to bark. The villagers kept the dogs for just that reason. Strangers were always a possible threat. The dogs were skinny creatures, for the only food given to them was the cobs discarded after the corn had been scraped off. The cobs were tossed on a midden in the yard to soften and molder to the proper consistency for the dogs to eat. It was the dogs who, years before, had alerted Maria's family so that Maria and her mother and little brother were able to escape the soldiers. How could Sarah face Maria and her mother? Because she was running from the guerrillas, would she be the enemy now? Sarah thought with fear that the men in the recording had come from this village, or, if not from this village, one nearby. And since this was the closest village, it would be the first place her captors would look. "I ought to go on," she told herself, but she knew she didn't have the strength.

While she stood there exhausted, undecided, the horizon lightened and a pale light flooded the village. Some of the village men stepped outside of their huts to see what had alerted the dogs. When they saw nothing they went back inside. The women were already up grinding maize for the breakfast *tortillas*. For a moment Sarah was carried back in time. She remembered how Maria had tried to teach her the trick of passing the dough through her fingers and from one hand to the other until the dough was so thin you could see through it. Sarah's dough always broke apart or came out lumpy and uneven.

Sarah was filled with a sudden and desperate desire to find Maria, even if Maria and her family turned her in. Quickly she skirted the village and came up behind Maria's house. A moment later she was dodging an inquiring dog and hurrying through the door of the Xelac house. Maria's mother, Juanita, let out a little scream and then when she saw the look on Sarah's face, clasped her hand over her mouth. In a rush of Mayan words, punctuated with Sarah's name, she asked in Spanish what had happened. "Your father? Your mother? Where are they? What are you doing here? You are like the little deer that suddenly appears from nowhere. Come, sit down, girl."

An old man appeared at the entrance of the hut and was staring at Sarah as though she were an apparition. Juanita drew him inside. "This is my second husband, Esteban," she said. "We have been married many years now."

Sarah sank onto a chair. "Maria?" she asked.

"Ah, Maria is married and has six children. Her husband is an overseer on the coffee plantation. He is paid every week and they have a house to themselves." There was pride in her voice.

"Maria is married to an overseer!"

"I know what you think. Many of them are brutes, but Maria's husband is a good man. She lives well with plenty for her and the children to eat. She even sends us food. We don't take sides now. We go our own way, for a friend one day is an enemy the next and the other way around as well. But, child, what are you doing here?"

Sarah looked at the man in the doorway suspiciously. Juanita said, "It is all right to speak in front of him."

Sarah gave him a quick, questioning look and then began to tell her story in a rush of words and tears. "They will be after me, I'm sure. They'll come here. I don't want to put you in danger."

Juanita tried to reassure her. "You are safe in our home...." Her husband strode over to Juanita and put a silencing hand on his wife's shoulder.

"But we must tell the others," he insisted. "This is something for the whole village. It could endanger us all."

"The guerrillas were once your friends," Sarah said.

"The guerrillas come and go," Juanita said. "They are our friends when it suits them. You are of our village. Your father was our friend. His medicine saved many lives."

"Won't it be dangerous to hide me?"

"Every day is dangerous here."

Sarah asked, "Do you have a phone in the village?"

"What would we do with a phone? We have only to walk out of our door to talk with someone. Tonight when it is dark we will take you to Maria. At the plantation they will know what to do. Now I must talk with the village."

Left alone with the man, Sarah tried to say a few words to him but Esteban only stared silently at her, as though it were impossible that words in his own language should come from the lips of someone like herself.

The dogs began to bark. Sarah ran to the window. An old

station wagon was speeding down the dusty track that led to the village, scattering chickens and dogs as it went. Maria's mother hurried into the house and Sarah felt herself pushed onto the floor and covered by a heap of quilts. There were shouts and then the sound of a man's angry voice. The voice grew closer and then was just outside the door. It was Carlos' voice demanding in Spanish to know if a white woman had been seen. Maria's mother answered in Mayan that she did not understand Spanish. *"Mujer, mujer,"* he snapped. *"Blanca."*

Sarah heard a man saying something. Sarah was sure it was Juanita's husband, Esteban, for Juanita was screaming for him to be silent, but now the quilts were being pulled away. Carlos grabbed Sarah and dragged her, shrieking, out of the house. When Juanita tried to stop them one of the men pushed her roughly to the ground. There were three men with Carlos, all with guns. The people of the village stood silently in front of their homes, watching.

Once in the car Carlos bound and gagged Sarah. "This time the ropes and gag will remain," he said. After a short ride Sarah was pulled out of the car and thrown down on a wooden floor. "There will be a guard here with you," he said. "This time we will not leave you alone. Anyhow it will not be for long. It seems you are not worth anything to either your family or your country. If you are expendable to them, you are expendable to us as well."

With her legs shackled by the ropes and her arms bound behind her back Sarah could do nothing. She was blindfolded and the tape on her mouth made it impossible to say that the ropes were cutting into her arms and legs. Outside she could hear someone walking back and forth. *I'm going to die,* Sarah thought, *"and I will never be able to tell Steve that I know what he did and that I forgive him and love him.* She could not bear to think of never again seeing the children. Over and over she prayed, "Dear Lord, let me see my children again." Hours passed, or maybe days. There was no way to tell. No one came to give her water or food. She knew if she were not given water she would only have a few days to suffer. Except for the terrible thirst, she almost wished that the water would be withheld so that her suffering would be over.

After the blackness of not being able to see and the silence of not being able to utter a word, the screams and shots were ear-splitting explosions. She was terrified that the next screams, silent screams, might be hers, the next shots meant for her. A door was forced open and she heard the voices of many men, among them Esteban's voice. Terrified, she thought, *They have come to kill me.*

Instead she felt her ropes cut and the gag and blindfold torn away. Opening her eyes she had trouble seeing at first. The world was nothing but bright flashing lights. Then there was Esteban smiling at her and with him several men—friendly men.

"Quickly," Esteban said in the Mayan dialect of the village. He picked her up and slung her over his shoulder. Moments later they were deep in some woods. He put her down. "Can you walk?" he asked.

Her legs were still numb from being bound, but Sarah nodded and began to walk, then to run as she followed Esteban and the other men. But the pace was too fast and the pain in her ankle unbearable. She sank down onto the ground. Esteban picked her up and carried her as if she were a child.

Flashing lights cut through the dark woods. The men sank down behind trees and bushes, avoiding the lights as if the lights might scorch them. In the distance they heard voices. The voices came closer and then began to recede. Still they waited. At last Esteban signaled the men to go on. They were out of the woods running toward a road where a car waited, its lights off. A door opened and Sarah was thrust inside. The last thing she saw before the car drove off was Esteban's smile.

The man next to her spoke Spanish. "I am Paco, Maria's husband," he said. "Juanita came to get me."

"I don't understand," Sarah said. "I thought Esteban was with the guerrillas. He told them where I was hiding."

"He knew the guerrillas would find out that the village hid you and then the whole village would pay. This way no one will know who it was who rescued you. The village has not forgotten the kindness of your parents. For them, you are of the village."

23

Steve sat with his hand on the phone. It had been four days. This morning even Evelyn had lost patience with him. She had suggested it might be best if he did not keep calling. But Steve insisted on talking to Benkin. "Trust me, Steve," the ambassador assured him, "we're doing everything we can. State has sent down a couple of men and the FBI are here as consultants. All very *sotto voce*, of course. If you come down here and start making a lot of noise the papers will get hold of it and that will only harden the guerrillas. They'll refuse to bargain. You have to understand our government is in a very delicate position. Right now we're in negotiations with the Costa Doran government on some human rights matters. If we can work out our differences, sanctions will be lifted and it will mean new markets for a lot of American businesses. The last thing we need is this story on all the front pages."

Steve exploded. "Sanctions! Business! Human rights! What about Sarah? What about her rights? If I don't hear anything by morning I'll be down there by tomorrow evening and I guarantee you the story will be on the front pages."

"Of course you are free to do what you want, Steve, but if you plan to give a story to the newspapers you might find they will be asking awkward questions about your past relationship with the guerrillas."

"If that's a threat, Benkin, I can tell you I don't care what the newspapers find out about me. I only care about Sarah."

He slammed down the receiver.

Now it was nearly dawn and Steve's hand was on the phone, the airline number before him. At first light he would call for reservations.

He could not remember when he had last slept. He was afraid of sleep, afraid of closing his eyes, afraid of not keeping a watch. He could not stop rehearsing his part in all of this. He had thought he understood what was going on in Costa Dora. He would not listen to Sarah's and his father's warnings that things were not as simple as he'd believed. Then his betrayal of his father led to his father's death. His sullen moods, his attempt to run away from his and Sarah's life at the university made Sarah go to Costa Dora. His contemptuous snub of Crites put Mia's life in danger. As far as he could see, everything he touched imperiled the lives of those he loved most. He watched the sky beginning to lighten in the east. He reached for the phone. But as he touched it, the phone came to life. He picked it up on the first ring.

"Steve, Jim Benkin here. I have some good news. Sarah is on her way home. I have the flight number."

Steve only took enough time to shout the news to his mother and hug the children who had run into the room at the sound of his elated voice. The five hour drive to the Detroit airport was a blur. His foot was on the accelerator, his hands on the steering wheel, his eye on the road, but all he could think of was how he would have to tell Sarah that he had betrayed his father. He saw now what hiding his terrible secret had done to their marriage. He had shut Sarah out of his life and had nearly lost her.

Steve was at the gate two hours early and though he couldn't remember when he had last eaten he couldn't leave. He bought a paper but it went unread. He could only sit there rehearsing what he would say to Sarah. But when he saw her plane taxi up to the gate he was unable to get out of his seat. He had nearly lost Sarah and now he might lose her again. He did not see how he could tell her the truth. But when she came through the door nothing mattered but getting his arms around her and never letting her go. He held her until she begged, "Steve, let me get my breath."

Reluctantly, Steve released her. "I can't believe you're here." He couldn't keep his voice from shaking. "I was coming down to Costa Dora today."

"The embassy wanted me to stay. They thought I ought to get a medical checkup and they wanted to question me but I could see they weren't anxious for the story to get out. I told them if I wasn't allowed to leave I'd tell the newspapers." Sarah smiled mischievously at Steve. "After that they literally rushed me onto a plane." The smile disappeared. "Steve, there's something I have to tell you."

"Whatever it is, it can wait...." He couldn't take his eyes from her. "I don't understand it. It's a miracle that you're here."

It was early evening and the usual business travelers had deserted the airport, giving it the feeling of a huge theater with no audience. Steve led Sarah into the airport restaurant which, except for a family with three small children who were enchanted with the whole idea of a cafeteria and couldn't stop choosing, was nearly empty. They took a table in a deserted corner. Steve could not let go of Sarah's hand. He did not think he would ever let go of her again. "Sarah, how did you get away? Did someone pay the ransom?"

"I was rescued." Steve listened, enraptured, as the story poured out.

" ... then Maria's husband took me by a back road to the coffee plantation. From there I was put on a small plane and flown to the city. After that the embassy took over. Oh, Steve, it was so good to see Maria! She's hardly changed and she has all these children. One of them is the age she and I were when we were friends. Steve, I'm sorry. If I hadn't gone away this would never have happened."

"If I hadn't been such a fool you never would have wanted to go away. Why did they pick you out to ... " He couldn't bring himself to say the word "kidnap."

"I wrote you about the wedding. I sent you the clipping from the paper with my picture. Carlos saw it. He sent me a letter."

"Carlos? You mean ... " Steve stared at her. He felt a cold chill. His father's assassin had sought out Sarah. "You didn't meet with him?"

"Yes. I had no idea why he wanted to see me and, after all, you had introduced me to him. I didn't know the story then."

"What story?"

"Steve, why didn't you trust me? Why didn't you tell me? Why did I have to learn it from him?"

At last Steve understood. "Carlos told you the information I gave him about my father led to my father's death. Is that what he said?"

Sarah nodded. "I wrote to you about the first century warrior we found, how priceless it was. Carlos wanted me to steal it and give it to the guerrillas so they could sell it and get the money they needed. If I didn't do it he said he would give out the story about why your father had been killed. Jean would find out and Dr. Abrabanel would find out. And, one day, the children. I knew it would devastate Jean and destroy any future you had with the university. I told myself it was only a statue, but you and Jean are flesh and blood."

Steve dropped her hand. Was there no end to the evil he had done? "Sarah, you didn't … "

"No. I planned to, but when the time came I couldn't. When I refused they kidnapped me. I wanted to get back before Carlos makes it all public. I thought Jean should hear it from us. Steve, how can we tell her something like that? It's impossible."

"Sarah, she knows. Something happened here the day you were kidnapped. I told her then. She's stronger than I ever imagined. I don't know if she has quite forgiven me, but at least she hasn't given up on me. I'm sure Carlos would have been malicious enough to send her a letter with the whole story. She would have believed it because she knew Dad's death wasn't a robbery. As for Dr. Abrabanel and the rest of the world, I promise you Carlos will never make the story public. Think what that would mean for the guerrillas. They would be exposed as assassins and kidnappers. They're trying to get recognition as a legitimate party on the ballot. If something like that got out it would ruin their chances. Carlos can't touch us."

Sarah was shivering. "Even if I had thought Carlos wouldn't tell anyone else but Jean, I couldn't have faced her knowing she knew the truth. But suppose I had actually stolen the statue to protect her and then had come home to find you had already told her! Oh, Steve."

Steve smiled grimly. "Not only would it be impossible for you to steal, but if you did, you would be terrible at it."

"Yes, I know. But why would Carlos think I could?"

"Because it was something he could have done. He would do anything for the revolution."

"Steve," Sarah asked in a voice that was nearly a whisper, "are you still on his side?"

Steve drew away from her. "How can you ask me that? A man who threatens my wife and kills my father. If I could get my hands on him I'd strangle him." He gave her an anguished look. "Sarah, that doesn't mean I don't care what happens to Costa Dora, to the people there. It only means I don't want their future in the hands of men like Carlos." He put his head in his hands. After a moment he looked at her. "I'm afraid I'm a deserter from the war that's going on down there. I have no heart for it."

He saw what his life would be like. He would return to the university and immerse himself in the academic world. He might even do well at it. He would be a good father and husband—and son. But the fire to help people, to change the world? That was gone. His impetuousness and pride had had terrible consequences, consequences he would have to live with for the rest of his life.

"Sarah, can you ever forgive me?"

"Yes. I forgave you long ago."

He shook his head. "Mother forgives me and you forgive me and somehow it might be possible that one day I might forgive myself, but I have the feeling that there is just so much forgiveness in the world and I've used it all up already."

"My father used to read the theologian, Kierkegaard. He said Kierkegaard taught him about love."

"Sarah, this is no time for abstract theology."

"No, listen to me, Steve. He said love believes everything and so is never deceived."

"That makes no sense."

"Yes, it does. You can't deceive someone who really loves you. If you really love someone, love includes everything about that person."

"I wish I could believe that," he said. "Sarah, how will I get through the rest of my life?"

"With me. Because I love you." Sarah looked closely at him. "Steve, you said something happened up north. What did you mean?"

"It was nothing. Mia was lost in the snow for a while."

"Steve, don't hide anything from me. I want to know exactly what happened."

"It was the opening of the hunting season. While the children were waiting for the school bus Mia saw Crites turn into our woods. She had heard me warn Crites to keep out of our woods. Instead of going to school, she took off after him. We found her and she's fine. She's probably still up. Call her and see for yourself. Do you want to spend the night here or … "

"I want to leave for home the minute after I talk with Mia and Tim. I don't care if we have to drive all night."

* * *

It was daylight when the children's voices woke Jean. Hastily she got out of bed and opened the door to prepare breakfast, only to find Steve and the children sitting around the table, eating. Confused, she asked, "Did you make breakfast, Steve?"

Mia giggled.

Tim said, "Mom made it."

Sarah walked in from the kitchen. In a minute Jean had her arms around her. "When did you get home?"

Steve was laughing. "About five this morning. We didn't want to wake you."

Sarah said, "We sat in the kitchen talking until the children woke up. Mia, Tim, get your coats on. The school bus will be along any minute."

Tim complained, "Mom, you just got here. Do we have to go to school today?"

"Yes, you do. I'll be here when you get home. I promise."

Tim, muffled into his down jacket, his face half hidden beneath his stocking cap, gave Sarah a lingering hug. Steve called after the children, "Mia, you and Tim stay right in front of the house." In the distance a large yellow shape materialized through the snow, red lights blinking like animal eyes. The three adults stood at the window watching until the red lights were turned off and the bus lumbered on, leaving an empty space at the road where the children had waited.

As she sat at the breakfast table listening to Sarah's story, Jean could hear the sound of yesterday's snow melting in the bright sun and dripping down from the eaves. The sun came through the window and flooded the room with light, wrapping itself like a warm shawl around her shoulders. She thought, *I'll never be afraid again that God will stop listening.* For a moment the warmth of the sun transported her back to the old capital. Sarah was describing the wedding she'd attended at the old capital. Jean had been to many such weddings. With Dan. For a moment, thinking of Dan, she stopped listening. What would Dan have said to all this? He had a large yardstick for measuring people. He had traveled too much and seen too much to judge people lightly. It was that quality that made him so valuable to the government. He could talk with anyone, listen to their side objectively, in any dispute find the shred of mutual need that might bring opposing sides together.

" ... if I would steal the statue for him," Sarah was saying.

"What!" Jean stared at Sarah.

"Of course I didn't. But I was so worried about Carlos telling you, and you already knew."

Jean laid her hand on Steve's arm. "I've just been thinking of Dan." She felt Steve's arm tighten under her hand but this had to be said. "I've thought of how he would have felt. He would have been angry, but he would have been forgiving. No, forgiving isn't the right word. There would have been no blame and so no need to forgive. He knew better than most men how weak we humans are. He always left judgment to God. If you believe anything else of your father, Steve, you are doing him an injustice."

To hide how much this speech had cost her Jean got up from the table to fill their coffee cups. "Now we have to get on with the rest of our lives. What are your plans?"

Steve looked at Sarah. Sarah said, "It was what we were talking about this morning. As soon as we can find a renter for the cabin we're going back to the university. Steve will work on his paper for the rest of this term and start teaching Spanish literature winter term. Dr. Abrabanel has always told him he could come back."

Steve said wryly, "I've decided to confine my ideas to the written word."

Sarah went on, "I want to write up some of our finds on the digs. The pottery had some really unique polychrome coloring."

"Jean," Sarah took her hand, "we want you to come back to the university with us. You'd make friends there in no time. They have a good museum. There's music. You can't want to go back to the old capital after all that's happened, and the two of us and the children would love to have you close by."

The words were exactly right, but Jean wasn't sure. Did they really want her? The chance to remain with Steve and Sarah and the children was hard to resist. She was beginning to see that she had been so wrapped up in Dan and their life together that she had neglected Steve. He had been a quiet child, solitary, polite, and if he had needed proof of her love, he would never have asked for it. Now she thought the best way to show she loved him would be to leave him alone, for she knew that every time Steve looked at her, he was reminded of Dan.

"I might take the cabin off your hands," she said. "For a few months. I have some thinking to do."

"You're not used to these winters," Steve warned her.

"Harry will keep an eye on me," she said, realizing Harry had never been far from her thoughts.

* * *

A week later a letter arrived for Jean from a border state in Mexico where the guerrillas were known to hide out during government crackdowns. Steve, who had picked up the mail, handed it to her like a man waiting to hear his death sentence pronounced.

There was no return address, yet Jean knew who had written it. She tried to think how she would have felt if Steve had not already told her. Coming in a letter the knowledge would have been devastating. Yet she would have known it was true. And then what? Would she have confronted Steve? Would she have remained silent and let the dreadful secret come between them for the rest of her life? Jean looked at Steve. She took the letter and threw it unopened into the fireplace.

24

The winter storms were a revelation to Jean, who had lived for years in countries where winter cold had been vanquished. The mornings in Michigan often began with a litany of school closings on the radio. The wind blew convulsively and the birds at the feeder hovered in midair as the gusts tossed them about. The crossroads were marked by great white humps, high as houses, the work of snowplows—no longer Steve's work.

Sarah called gratefully from the university downstate. "Steve is his old self again. I have you to thank for that, Jean. When are you coming down for a visit? The children miss you. We all do."

Jean listened carefully for any sign that there was still trouble in their marriage, but Sarah's voice was open, relaxed.

Harry came to visit each day. She watched from the cabin window as he made his way through the snow from his pickup, his head raised and his mouth slightly open to taste the freshness of the snow. After what she had experienced this past year his innocence frightened her. He brought in firewood and shoveled the driveway so she could get out the truck, which Steve had left for her and which she enjoyed driving. She liked the height from which you saw things and the rough, bucking ride that confirmed with every bump her belief that getting from one place to another was arduous.

On clement days Jean and Harry snowshoed through the woods. Jean was delighted at the novelty of moving over the top of the snow-covered brush. "It's like walking on water," she wrote to Tim and Mia. Evenings in the darkened cabin with no illumination but the fire, she and Harry told each other about their lives.

"What was it like to spend so much of your childhood around a museum?" Harry wanted to know one evening.

"I liked going there with my father when the museum was closed to visitors and I had it all to myself." She had never owned anything as she had owned those deserted rooms. "The paintings and sculptures were more alive when people weren't there. People seemed to make them hold back."

"My childhood was the opposite of yours," Harry said. "I was never indoors. In Germany, where my father came from, a man like him would never have been able to buy a large piece of property. He could hardly believe his luck when he came here. And another thing that surprised him: in this country, no one owned the rivers. He got the idea of working as a guide. There were a lot of wealthy sportsmen coming up to trout fish. It seemed such an easy way to make money. He thought he'd discovered an incredible secret and he was determined to teach me everything he knew so I could have the same life he had. I grew up on the river."

* * *

In February there was an ice storm and the electricity went off for two days, shutting down the furnace and water pump. At night Jean slept in a sleeping bag next to the fireplace. On the second day of the storm Harry came over to bring in wood so the fireplace would keep the cabin warm.

"The Valhallists must be loving this," Harry said. "It's what they've been waiting for—something to go wrong. They can use all their bottled water and their freeze-dried food. I don't know how they managed it, but they seem to be blaming the power outage on some racial plot. I'll tell you what else they are up to. They're trying to dam up the stream that flows through their property and empties into the river." Harry's voice rose. "It's an outrage. I've been on the phone to the state and I'm going to write a series of editorials about the Valhallists."

A week later the Valhallists retaliated. Harry found the tires of his pickup slashed. The following week there was sand in his gas tank. That was nothing compared to their next assault. Harry awoke in the night to the sound of a shot. In the morning only two owls came to be fed. They were skittish, afraid of Harry. They took the food he offered, but they carried it away instead of devouring it while he looked on, as they usually did. "I don't know what hurts the most—the death of one of the owls," he said to Jean in a mournful voice, "or the distrust of the two that are left."

In the midst of the trouble with the Valhallists Jean received a phone call from Steve. "I've been asked to give a paper at the *Universidad de Costa Dora.* Any old friends you'd like me to look up?"

Jean could not help herself. "Steve, you can't really be thinking of going back there?" She gripped the receiver with something that was close to panic. Was there to be no safety anywhere for those she loved?

"Don't worry, Mother. It's only for a few days, and I'll be far from the guerrillas."

"They have connections everywhere."

"I'm no use to them now. They'll leave me alone. It's a great opportunity—I can't pass it up. I'll look up Dr. Jansen for you and call you and give you all the news about the clinic when I get back." Jean hung up the phone feeling helpless to protect those she loved.

That night she had her first quarrel with Harry. It was over his editorials against the Valhallists. "I spent half a lifetime worrying about Dan and then Steve," Jean said. "I'm tired of men with causes."

"Jean, you know I'm not the kind of man to go looking for a fight, but I won't turn away from one, either. I can't believe there's a person alive who isn't prepared to fight for something."

"Then let someone else do the crusading. What's a river compared with your safety? There are thousands of rivers. We can find another one."

Harry's face, pale and naked without its summer tan, crumpled. He left the cabin without a word. Jean was furious with herself for attacking Harry, furious with Harry for not fighting back. At least if he'd fought back his angry words might have cancelled out her spiteful ones.

A seemingly endless week went by, and still Jean heard nothing from Harry. The paper carried another editorial about the Valhallists. Alone in the cabin, nagged by the howling winds and sleet pelting her window, Jean recognized the irrational tantrum for what it was—a last defense against what she finally had to admit was her love for Harry. She couldn't imagine life without him. Worrying about the people you love, as she had worried about Dan and now about Steve and Harry, is a condition of life she realized. If she never worried, it would be because there was no love in her life, and that would be intolerable.

She had to see Harry. She thought of driving to his cabin but her driveway was covered with a thick blanket of snow. In the woods the tree branches bent under their burdens. Jean picked up the phone to call Harry but the line was dead.

She bundled up in an old jacket and cap of Steve's and began to shovel several days' accumulation of snow from the driveway. The wet snow was heavy and seemed to pile up faster than she could shovel it. Her shoulders began to ache and there was a pain in her chest. Still she kept on shoveling, desperate to tell Harry how she felt. Then the pain began to take on a life of its own, squeezing her chest until she felt as though some giant had gripped her in his arms and was crushing her to death. She started for the cabin, knowing there was no way to call an ambulance, but not wanting to die alone in the snow. Halfway to the cabin she slipped and fell. There was no getting up. "Dear God," she prayed, "don't let me die in this coldness."

* * *

When she awoke she saw that everything around her was still white. But it was not the white of snow but the white of hospital sheets and walls. She was warm beneath blankets. Her hand was in someone else's hand, Harry's hand. She heard him say, "Maybe you'd be willing to keep me around to shovel your driveway."

She smiled weakly. "The job is yours. How did you find me?"

"I tried to call you but the line was down. I worried that your electricity was out again so I took off. When I got there you were nearly covered with snow." In spite of his efforts to keep his voice light, his hoarseness gave away his fright. "I put you into the car and drove ninety miles an hour to the hospital. The sheriff was after me but he couldn't catch up. His siren kept the road clear." Harry tried a small smile and squeezed her hand. "What were you doing out there?"

"I was on my way to your cabin to tell you what a fool I had made of myself." She looked up at him. "When can I get out of here?"

"The doctor says in a day or two. They want to do a few tests. Hadn't I better call Steve?"

"No, please. Steve is due to go back to Costa Dora for some meeting on Latin American literature. He knows I don't want him to go and he'll think this is my way of keeping him home. Harry, I'm through trying to tell the people I love how to live their lives; I'm even going to try not to worry about them. You can write all the editorials you want." She remembered her answered plea to God to keep her from dying in the coldness. Now she would ask him to watch over Harry and Steve.

Harry looked down at her and smiled. "I don't want to take advantage of your weakness but I had a word with the hospital chaplain. He said he'd be glad to marry us. Then you could come home with me so I could keep an eye on you."

Jean was speechless but only for a moment. "Only if you promise it isn't always winter here."

"I promise. Spring is almost here. I saw the snow fleas hopping around today and one of the owls got a red-winged blackbird."

"Fleas and dead blackbirds. How inviting!" Jean laughed.

Harry was right. It turned out to be the warmest March on record. The snow dwindled into white tags and patches. Then one mild day it vanished altogether. The children sent homemade wedding gifts. Mia wove identical friendship bracelets for Jean and Harry. Tim drew a picture of Harry and Jean in a canoe and framed it in cardboard which he had covered with foil. Steve called to say the paper had been a success and he was safely home.

"Dr. Jansen is fine, and the clinic is doing well. She's had a gift of money and she's adding a new wing. She wouldn't say where the money was coming from but the check appears to have arrived the day after you sold your house in the old capital. I don't suppose there's any connection?"

"No comment," was her reply.

Jean heard Steve laugh. She was just breathing a sigh of relief when Steve went on to say, "We may send the children up for a few weeks this summer, though, and ask you to babysit. They want Sarah back at the dig and a new democratic party is gaining a lot of support. It has nothing to do with the guerrillas and nothing to do with the army. The leaders of the party are anxious to establish good relations with the States. I may go down with Sarah and help the party with translating. And I still have embassy contacts."

Jean thought her heart would surely stop. She was about to plead with Steve not to return to Coast Dora when Steve said, "I think Dad would approve of my approach this time."

Jean saw that for Steve this was a kind of atonement, a resolution to his ongoing argument with Dan. Whatever it cost her she couldn't deny him this consolation.

At the end of April the trout season opened. Jean suggested she and Harry take a trip on the river. They launched their canoe into a stream swollen with melting snow. The snags and sandbars that had been hazards in the autumn's shallow waters were now easily cleared. A blue heron watched them from his perch on a log. As the warm air settled onto the still-frozen ground a thick layer of fog covered the river.

It was noon by the time they reached the camp of the Valhallists. The sun was burning jagged orange holes through the fog. There were no sentries on duty. The buildings they had guarded were deserted.

Jean and Harry beached the canoe and wandered through the abandoned camp. The Valhallists must have shivered in their poorly-made cabins. Their root cellar had not been dug deeply enough and their vegetables had frozen. A deer carcass lay near the cellar, clumsily dressed out. Harry said the meat must have been tainted and inedible. Defeated by the winter, the Valhallists had moved away into other people's lives. They had not discovered, as Jean had, that it was possible to outlast, to outstay the cold.

Harry promised that in a month the woods would be filled with flowers: spring beauties, Dutchman's-breeches, trout lilies, and trailing arbutus—all making the most of the sun before the leaves broke out overhead to spread their many small shadows.

ANOTHER TALE OF POLITICAL INTRIGUE
BY GLORIA WHELAN

The President's Mother

*When the president threatens to jeopardize thousands of innocent lives,
one woman will risk everything to stop him.
And the White House will do anything to silence her.*

When President Robert Lange tries to push a cost-cutting health care bill through Congress that would deny necessary medical care to the elderly and infirm, his mother tries to dissuade him. Concerned that she will expose his biggest secret, the president has her put away, then hires an aging actress to take his mother's place. An imaginative tale of political intrigue that explores the horrific consequences of misplaced power. *$10.99*